CARDINAL POINTS LITERARY JOURNAL
VOLUME 11

a project of
the *Slavic Studies Department, Brown University*
and
StoSvet
www.StoSvet.net

ISBN: 9798472848213

Published by StoSvet Press
www.StoSvet.net/lib
cp@StoSvet.net

CARDINAL POINTS

THE LITERARY JOURNAL
OF THE SLAVIC STUDIES DEPARTMENT,
BROWN UNIVERSITY

VOLUME 11

in dear

Hugh and Lotti

from Dralyuk

EDITED BY BORIS DRALYUK

DEDICATED TO THE DE-STALINIZATION OF THE AIR

StoSvet Press
New York, New York

CONTENTS

6

PROSE

A Writer is Born
An Excerpt from The *Devil at Large in Moscow:*
The Life of Mikhail Bulgakov[1]

Homero Freitas de Andrade

Translated from the Portuguese
by Kevin Windle

The year was 1891. Famine stalked the Empire of Tsar Alexander III. Bad harvests came one after another even in the traditionally fertile regions of the South and West of the vast Empire of All the Russias. The autocratic state was making a determined effort to expand its territory and industrialize by means of foreign investment. In the previous decade, industrial production had increased significantly, creating an illusion of prosperity. The agrarian crisis was aggravated by a policy which, in order to repay the rising foreign debt, put a premium on the export of already diminished agricultural output. The nobility and the capitalists waxed richer. The peasants, emancipated thirty years earlier, went hungry as they struggled to pay the punitive taxes imposed on them. In the big cities, while the upper echelons of the bureaucracy traded influence as usual, and titular counselors sat and cultivated their haemorrhoidal complexions in the same offices as before, the workers struck for higher wages and discussed their rights, and as a result political awareness increased in the industrial proletariat as a class.

Afanasy Ivanovich Bulgakov, a lecturer in theology, who had recently arrived in Kiev with his wife from Karachev, in the province of Orel,[2] where they had married the previous year, spent his days teaching ancient history at a college for daughters of the Kiev nobility. Varvara Mikhailovna Pokrovskaya-Bulgakova[3] was awaiting the birth of their first son in a house in Novo-Gospitalnaya Street. Mikhail, their first-born, named after the patron saint of the city and his maternal grandfather, was born on May 15 (May 3 by the Julian calendar).

---

1   *O Diabo Solto em Moscou: A Vida do Senhor Bulgákov* (São Paulo, 2002).

2   "Orlov" in the original is incorrect. (*Trans.*)

3   "Prokóvskaia" in the original is incorrect. (*Trans.*)

Afanasy Bulgakov (1859-1907), eldest son of an Orthodox priest and scion of the minor nobility, native of the city of Orel, had completed his theological studies in 1885 at the Kiev Theological Academy. After graduation, he taught Greek in a seminary in Novocherkassk while preparing his Master's dissertation. In addition to classical languages, he knew English, German and French well, and read Old Church Slavonic texts in the original. After completing his Master's degree, he joined the academic staff of the Kiev Theological Academy and proceeded to a doctorate in theology in 1906. Varvara Bulgakova (1869-1922), the daughter of an arch-priest in the cathedral of Karachev, completed her school education in her home town and for two years before marriage taught fourth-year classes in the local girls' school. After Mikhail, other children followed: Vera (1892), Nadezhda (Nadia, 1893), Varvara (Varia, 1895), Nikolai (Kolia, 1898), Ivan (Vania, 1900), and Elena (Lelia, 1902).

Their father, who paid close attention to the care of his children, played the violin in his spare time and sang in his deep bass voice. Their mother, who played Chopin on the piano to her children at bedtime, was a jolly and cheerful soul with a ready smile. Both parents were of Russian background, and although they might sometimes use Ukrainian in day-to-day matters they gave their children an essentially Russian upbringing. They did not live a life of luxury, but were comfortably off. A monarchist with liberal ideas, Afanasy Bulgakov raised his children in accordance with the precepts of the Orthodox Church, although their house on Andreevsky Hill, to which the family had moved after a short period in Kudriavskaya Street, was frequented by intellectuals and academics, representatives of the intelligentsia of Kiev, and was never a highly religious environment. Only the customary rituals were observed: church services, Lent and Christmas.

By the age of seven Mikhail had learned to read and write. Like all the other members of his family, he became an avid reader. He delighted in the *Baba Yagas* and *Leshies* of Russian fairy tales,[4] many of which he had heard from his mother in

---

4   *Baba Yaga*: traditional witch figure in Russian folktales for children. *Leshy*: wood nymph.

the evenings. According to a list found among the documents and other materials comprising the family archive assembled by his sister Nadia, his own first story, "The Adventures of Svetlan," dates from this period. Nadia did not think that it was worthy of publication, but he did at least set it down, having been in the habit of composing orally.[5] By the turn of the century his bedtime reading was Gogol's novel *Dead Souls*.

In 1901, after a preparatory year, Mikhail entered Kiev's Grammar School No. 1, which would later provide the setting for some passages of his novel *The White Guard*. Many of the teachers taught or had previously taught at the university. According to his classmate E. B. Bukreev, as a schoolboy Bulgakov was "a great one for teasing, and invented nicknames for everybody."[6] The writer Konstantin Paustovsky, who attended the same school, remembered him as one who was always getting into fights.[7] A diligent student, with few friends other than those who also formed part of the family circle, he never stood out in school life. As Bukreev reports,

> *In our fifth year we formed various discussion groups, on economics, philosophy and religion. Bulgakov never joined any of them. [...] In that year the events of 1905 overtook us. We of course smashed windows and threw inkwells about. Bulgakov joined in, as he did in all group activities of that kind. Of course it was great fun to barricade the doors and not let the teachers in. We also elected a school community soviet, with one or two representatives from each year. I recall meetings in people's apartments, where we lay around on beds smoking and making fiery speeches ... That was as far as it went. Bulgakov never played any part at all in any soviets or meetings. Total anarchy, complete chaos reigned at our school for two or three weeks, then things settled down. Thanks to the headmaster, E. A. Bessmertny, none of the pupils suffered any consequences.*[8]

---

5   E. A. Zemskaia, "Iz semeinogo arkhiva," in E. Bulgakova and S. Liandres (eds.), *Vospominaniia o Mikhaile Bulgakove* (Moscow, 1988), 47.

6   Bukreev quoted in M. Chudakova, *Zhizneopisanie Mikhaila Bulgakova* (Moscow, 1988), 14. [Here and below, the English translation is from the original Russian. *Trans.*]

7   Ibid., 19.

8   Ibid., 20.

The events of 1905 may be considered the first practical result of a protracted effort by the intelligentsia, initiated some years after the rout of the Decembrist rising in 1825,[9] to raise popular awareness of the need for political change. If for the Right the movement represented yet another failure for those who dared to rise up against the power and prerogatives of the autocrats, for the parties of the Left and center Left it served as a kind of dress rehearsal for a future revolution. Aging Populists (*Narodniki*), Social Democrats, Social Revolutionaries, anarchists, and even some more enlightened sections of the bourgeoisie, while not achieving their immediate objectives in the struggle against Tsarism, succeeded in severely shaking the foundations of the Empire, which had already been eaten away by poverty, famine, foreign debt, the ongoing agrarian crisis, the oppression of national minorities, defeat in the war with Japan, etc. At the same time, the outside world and the fearful eyes of the nobility and the bourgeoisie, with its *sauve-qui-peut* attitude, saw only the official stereotype of a miracle of industrialization and progress of the peoples of Russia.

According to Marc Ferro, the failure of the 1905 revolution showed that, left to itself, the working class could achieve little, and that the peasantry were not yet sufficiently mature for any large-scale political action.[10] In any event, be it due to social insurrection or the ideological confrontations which shook old Russia out of the apathy in which it was wallowing, 1905 left deep scars on the daily life of its big cities and on the generation then being formed. For example, the strikes, riots and demonstrations in the most liberal grammar schools and the universities of the Empire were so serious and persistent that the government rejoiced when the trouble died down. Repression had to show a kinder face in order to avoid aggravating the situation. Bukreev goes on,

> *In 1905, in our fifth year, I was a convinced anarchist. I had the best library on anarchism in Kiev, including all of Kropotkin. In the Kreshchatik, near the*

---

9   Decembrist rising: a rebellion by army officers who refused to take an oath of allegiance to the new emperor Nicholas I on his accession in December 1825. [...]

10 Marc Ferro, *La Révolution russe de 1917* (Paris, 1967).

corner of Fundukleevskaya Street, a dentist called Lurye had a first-floor flat, and the living room was given over to the anarchists. Anarchist literature lay all over the tables, and anybody who wanted could come along and read it.[11]

But what part did Bulgakov play in all this, and what was his position, if he had one at all?

One needs to realize that in his schooldays Bulgakov was an utterly uncompromising monarchist, a chauvinist. [...] The monarchists came from very wealthy families, usually landed families, and from the urban lower class with "Black-Hundred" tendencies. Bulgakov did not share that crude strain, but of course on the whole our school was known for being more liberal, compared to others, so there weren't very many even of his kind. Generally speaking, the school had a concentration of mutually opposing views. [...] Bulgakov was not among the out-and-out "Black Hundreds," of course. You could say that he held Rightist views, but of a moderate kind.[12]

It was not only his political immaturity that determined his carefree, not to say aloof, demeanor with regard to the social events of the era. The home and his family were still the focus of his attention and the stage on which he performed. As a youth he had a passion for football, a game only recently introduced to Kiev. He dreamed of one day becoming an opera singer, with his fine baritone voice. He staged drawing-room skits and playlets. He organized performances which he wrote or adapted himself. With his brothers and sisters and friends, he staged them in the park at Bucha, a village thirty kilometers from Kiev, where the family had built a *dacha*. For family soirées he would write satirical farces and improvise scenes featuring the family. He drew cartoons, played the piano and sang. And he read. He turned the house into a forum for discussion of the burning issues of the day: the woman question, the British suffragettes, hypnotism, the Ukrainian question, Tolstoy's theory of non-violence and Nietzsche's superman.

All in all, with his mother, whose laughter echoed through the house all day

---

11   Chudakova, *Zhizneopisanie*, 21.
12   Ibid., 21-22.

long, he set the tone of day-to-day humor which formed the perfect counterweight to the seriousness and rigor in which the family were raised. He was never an *enfant terrible*, at least not in the primary sense of the term. His rebelliousness showed itself in fully developed form in his skits based on the home life of his family and circle of friends.

At this time, perhaps, his persona as actor and writer was taking shape, if we bear in mind his sister Nadia's memory of his jokes and catch-phrases becoming proverbial and entering the language of the family.[13] [...]

1906 and 1907 were difficult years for the Bulgakovs. Afanasy Bulgakov received his doctorate in theology in 1906, while still working as censor of works in German, English and French, earning an annual salary of approximately 2,000 roubles. However, in the spring of that year he fell ill with a serious and chronic disease of the kidneys, the same ailment which years later would cause the death of his son. It progressed rapidly, forcing him to retire in March 1907 from the Theological Academy, where he was one of the most highly regarded professors. Less than a week later he died, handing on to Varvara Bulgakova's energetic shoulders the burden of responsibility for running the family.

Bulgakov's reaction to his father's death is unknown. It is somewhat surprising, moreover, that the family archive, the principal biographies and the recollections of his contemporaries make no mention at all of the nature of the relationship between father and son. The more surprising since they tell of the closeness between mother and son, and the bond between Bulgakov and his sister Nadia. We may suppose that his relations with his father were cordial though not particularly intimate, and that he – as was natural, given his age and temperament – accepted paternal authority without question, in accordance with the moral and religious standards of his upbringing. Later, while working on his novel *The Master and Margarita*, he would consult his father's articles and essays on the history of Christianity. Other works would feature the recurring image of the green lampshade

---

13   Quoted in Zemskaia, *Vospominaniia*, 21.

by which his father used to write and which Bulgakov associated with scholarly discipline and creative work. However, when his father died, his role in the family changed.

When routine was re-established in the house on Andreevsky Hill, two young cousins and an aunt joined the household. To eke out the budget the older brothers gave private lessons. Varvara Bulgakova took charge of rearing the younger children. The atmosphere became jolly once again. Evenings were given over to chess, charades, improvisations, playlets, and singing and dancing. (Mikhail was ever able to invent new forms of entertainment.) In summer, at Bucha, they played football, cricket and tennis. In winter they went skiing. They visited public parks and began to go to the city's theaters. Opera became a shared passion. Feodor Chaliapin often performed in Kiev. We know that, by the time he graduated from the university, Bulgakov had attended forty-one performances of Gounod's *Faust*, whose theme he would recreate in his masterpiece *The Master and Margarita*.

At the age of seventeen Bulgakov made the acquaintance of Tatiana Niko-laevna Lappa (1889-1982),[14] the daughter of a well-to-do aristocratic family. She had arrived in Kiev from Saratov to spend the summer with her grandmother and aunt, both of whom were friendly with Varvara Bulgakova. Mikhail was enlisted to show her the city. They took long walks together and eventually fell in love. This was Bulgakov's first love. Instead of returning to Saratov, Tatiana went to Moscow at the end of the year. For Bulgakov the separation was painful and he threatened suicide.[15] Distance and the difficulty of meeting complicated their romance, which they continued in an exchange of frequent long letters.

In mid-1909 Mikhail completed his schooling. He may not have stood out for his academic progress, but was well liked for his wicked sense of humour and his creativity. He continued to develop his humorous streak, writing satirical verse

---

14   Dates as given. All other sources indicate that Tatiana Lappa was born in 1892. (*Trans.*)

15   See the transcription of an interview with Tatiana Lappa in V. Vozdvizhenskii (ed.), *Mikhail Bulgakov i ego vremia* (Moscow, 1990), 15. Also in *Vospominaniia*.

and cutting epigrams, as well as plays. He wrote or adapted, directed and acted. The posters which the brothers distributed in Bucha that summer advertised a varied program for the "season." It opened with "The Seance" (subtitled "People of nervous disposition are asked not to attend"), a ballet in verse composed by a friend of the family. Mikhail was responsible for the direction and played the role of medium. This was followed by the vaudeville "Granny's Will," in which he played the fiancé, a naval officer. The season ended with "The Jubilee" and "The Proposal," both by Anton Chekhov.

As family entertainment (and education), the music, the games, the theatricals and improvisations which enlivened their Saturday evenings in the house on Andreevsky Hill took second place only to their daily reading. According to Nadia Bulgakova, all were fanatical readers and knew their Russian literature very well.[16]

[...]

Soon, however, assailed by doubts about religion and religious faith, Bulgakov began to abandon the family's practice of religious observance, beginning with Lent and Easter communion. He provoked heated debate with his brothers, sisters, and friends, setting religion against science. He upheld Darwin's theories and in time arrived at an atheist position – which he dropped only in the last decade of his life. Following the example of Chekhov, and perhaps influenced by his mother, whose three brothers were doctors, Bulgakov opted for a career in medicine and entered the University of Kiev in September 1909. Kiev was then being shaken by waves of nationalism, which led to fierce debate among the students on the question of the "Ukrainianization" of Ukraine. Bulgakov opposed it: he regarded Kiev and Kievan Rus as the mother of Muscovite Russia and of Russia itself. However, these debates did not fire the first-year student with enthusiasm; when the social and political ills of the Empire were being ventilated in public (outside the home), he tended to beat a timid retreat. He would spend hours on end at his microscope, or dissecting animals, or carefully trapping butterflies and insects for a collection

---

16 See *Vospominaniia*, 57-58.

which he would donate to the university in 1916, aware of its value to science.

The news of the death of Leo Tolstoy in 1910 plunged Kiev and all of Russia into mourning. Demonstrations followed throughout the city, especially in university circles. According to Bulgakov's friends and relations, Tolstoy's death affected him deeply; he regarded him as the greatest Russian writer of the period, and was attracted by his idea of meeting violence with non-violent resistance. Nonetheless, he held aloof from any form of agitation. Some students were arrested and sentenced. The situation was so tense that in January 1911 the Council of Ministers decided to terminate the autonomy of higher educational institutions and ban meetings of students in the universities. The students reacted immediately, and the University of Kiev launched a strike which went on until the beginning of April. Bulgakov was irked by the paralysis of academic work: he wanted to complete his studies, receive his degree, find a position, and above all see Tatiana, for whom he could only express his love by letter.

While his non-participation meant that Bulgakov was coming to be seen as an outsider, if not a reactionary, this does not mean that he really was one. On the contrary, he observed what was happening around him with a keen and astute eye, as his diaries, stories and novels describing the events of the period would later show. His own position already seems to have been that of a third-person narrator, one who simply observes and describes, without taking any direct part in the action.

Be that as it may, Bulgakov's university years (1909-1916) were extremely unsettled. On the one hand there were the serious socio-political problems of the Empire, which led to frequent outbreaks of disturbances and strikes and interrupted the continuity of academic life. On the other, affairs of the heart left him restless, when he did not miss classes to follow Tatiana to Saratov. At Christmas 1911, he was introduced to Tatiana's parents. "We had a Christmas party. We danced and spent most of the time in amorous conversation," Tatiana Lappa recalled.[17] In the

---

17   *Vospominaniia*, 111.

summer of 1912 he was a guest in her home, and together they travelled to Kiev, she on the pretext of studying the history of Romance and Germanic languages in Kiev. As she would admit, this was no more than an excuse.[18] [...]

She did not complete her course. Her romance with Bulgakov consumed all her spare time as well as his. She told of symphony concerts in the Kupechesky Gardens and Bulgakov's love for the overtures to *Ruslan and Ludmila* and *Aïda*. [...][19]

At a railway station, on one of the occasions when he was returning from Saratov, an elderly gypsy woman read his palm and predicted that he would soon be married. She added that his future held not one marriage, but three. Being superstitious, he believed her. However, an unwanted pregnancy and subsequent abortion may have expedited matters.[20] The fact remains that Bulgakov unleashed a veritable storm in the family: his siblings and parents were divided. Varvara Bulgakova advised Tatiana not to marry until Mikhail graduated. Her son,[21] however, was determined. He wrote a skit about the situation.[22] Finally, after much pressure, the happy ending came to pass on April 26, 1913, with a simple ceremony, not well attended, in the Church of St Nicholas on Andreevsky Hill, followed by tea, fruit and refreshments in the home of the bridegroom's mother.

At first, the couple remained at the same address. The family's Saturday evening entertainments, as in their childhood, continued to be very lively, especially in winter, when Mikhail invented a new game, the "pantomime charade." By this time, after a brief period in Retarskaya Street, they had their own room with a separate entrance, facing the church in which they had married. When not at the university, where he was a diligent and dedicated student, Bulgakov pursued research in the public library. When not in either of these places, he was

18   Interview with L. Parshin, "Ego pervaia liubov'," *LG-dos'e* 5 (1991), 4.
19   *Vospominaniia*, p. 111.
20   See *Zhizneopisanie*, 55, and Parshin, 4. [...]
21   See Parshin, 4. [...]
22   The piece was entitled "S miru po nitke – golomu shish." [...]

with Tatiana in the cafés and restaurants of a city where good times were in plentiful supply. They went to concerts, the theater and the cinema. They spent all the money they had received from Bulgakov's father-in-law, as well as the little he earned from private lessons. Varvara Bulgakova was sternly critical of their frivolity.[23] Wedding rings and jewellery were kept permanently at the pawnbroker's. Friends would appear late at night with a small gift for Tatiana, saying, "Tasia, while you're eating these sweets, we're going to play billiards with Misha."[24]

The Russian Empire, in the grip of social tension, financial speculation and corruption at all levels of the state apparatus, along with the moral and intellectual impoverishment of the middle classes and the wretched state of the rest of the population, entered the war in August 1914 with an offensive, initially successful, in East Prussia.

> *The Russian advance was halted at the battle of Tannenberg (August 23-31, 1914), and, as the war progressed, the Germans counter-attacked until they occupied a line running west of Petersburg roughly from Orsha to Kharkov and thence to Rostov. The German object was to divide up Russian-held territory into its alleged "natural" components, i.e. to deprive Russia of Poland, Lithuania, the Baltic provinces, Finland and above all the Ukraine, which was then to be made dependent on Germany. The intention was to limit the Russian Empire to the Great Russian territories, and to isolate it especially from the sea.*[25]

The outbreak of war caught Bulgakov and his wife by surprise in Saratov in August 1914. Tatiana's mother established an infirmary for soldiers wounded in action, and Bulgakov was able to practice what he had learned until classes resumed at the university. When they returned to Kiev, he took up his studies again while she went to work as a nurse in a hospital. Their friends were soon being called up. These included Boris Bogdanov, their closest friend, a regular and brilliant participant in their Saturday performances. He had paid court to Varia

---

23   See Vozdvizhenskii, *Mikhail Bulgakov i ego vremia* (Moscow, 1990), 16.

24   Ibid., 46.

25   Otto Hoetzsch, *The Evolution of Russia*, trans. from the German by Rhys Evans (London, 1966), 181. [Title and text corrected, *Trans.*]

Bulgakova, and when faced by her rejection and his recruitment for the front, shaved off his moustache in protest.

Shortly before he was due to depart for the front in February 1915, Bogdanov would be the focus of a tragic event which left Bulgakov – who played a supporting role in the dreadful scene – with scars that can be seen in certain passages of his later narrative prose.[26] One day Bulgakov received a note from Bogdanov, whom he had not seen for a while, asking him to come urgently to his home. When he arrived, he found Bogdanov lying in bed. Bulgakov wanted to smoke but had come without any cigarettes. "Take mine from my coat pocket," said Bogdanov. Bulgakov rummaged in one pocket and found only one kopeck. At that moment he heard a shot. He turned and saw his friend drenched in blood, a Browning pistol slipping from his grasp. Despite all his efforts, he could not save him. Later a note was found in the cigarette packet: "Nobody is to blame for my death."

The times were changing just as rapidly as the scenes in the film *The Picture of Dorian Gray*, which Meyerhold had recently shot and which was premiering to great popular acclaim.[27] The glow of a languid *belle époque* that lit up the specious veneer of prosperity in the realm of All the Russias was fading. In August the situation at the front was catastrophic. The Germans had just taken Lutsk, opening the way to Kiev with the intention of seizing it and withdrawing along the Dnieper. Kiev, for its part, resembled a refugee camp. The residents of the city sent their children away. The university suspended lectures. Only the Faculty of Medicine continued to function until April 1916, training its students for front-line service. Bulgakov passed all his examinations and graduated, got drunk for the first time and set out the next day to enrol as a doctor in the Red Cross, starting work in the Kiev hospital. The Russian offensives intensified to the point where Lutsk was recaptured from the Germans. With the advance, the hospitals were moved closer to the front. Bulgakov was transferred to Chernovtsy, fifty kilometers from the battlefields.

26 Above all in "Morphine" ("Morfii," in Mikhail Bulgakov, *Izbrannoe* [Moscow, 1982], 346-370). [...]
27 See Jay Leyda, *Kino: A History of the Russian and Soviet Film* (London, 1973), 81.

Lying to Ourselves

Zsuzsa Hetényi

Last year, during the first wave of the pandemic, I was one of several writers invited to answer 3+1 questions by a Hungarian literary journal litera.hu. I was surprised that only three of us responded. My own answers were very nearly ready even before I was asked, and they stayed with me because they were by no means merely "side effects" provoked by the virus.

What has happened to us? (1)

What is time? What is death? And who is that sympathetic creature I'm living with, that is to say, myself? During the first week, these were the three issues that preoccupied me whatever I was doing.

Suddenly everything came into focus, clear, and sharp. Not least because I finally started to wear the glasses I was prescribed two years ago (they allegedly protect the eyes' mucous membranes from infection). It was remarkable to see how whoever was good got even better, and anyone who was evil appeared even more warped. The extrovert became more extro, the introvert became even more intro, the depressive plunged into the lower depths, the manic rushed around more dementedly. Hardly anyone on the street maintained social distancing and often came aggressively close. Gray hair was a provocation, if not an actual target.

We are overwhelmed by the political lies towering above us, the dictatorship that has congealed around us. The contagious "Other" dons the phantoms of the enemy's image. The military operetta state has indeed got on its high horse.

While they are lying to us so comprehensively, we must nevertheless ask in the end how we are lying to ourselves. It's a great opportunity to gain self-knowledge.

In the first few days I would have hurried to help out, but I realized there was no going anywhere, so all that remained was making donations. I was made speechless by the realization that I had become an endangered species several times over, and that now it would rather be I who would be offered help. Quite a few of my former students called me and offered to help with my shopping: this was indescribably uplifting, and I recall it daily with joy and grateful thanks.

If the end was now indeed nigh, I'd have time for everything, I thought. The calendar was clear and it opened the floodgates. The airplane was flying ever faster, but now the engine had stopped abruptly mid-air and millions of us are floating in the deafening silence, suspended above a gaping abyss. Freedom and fear.

The outlines of my new life took shape almost immediately, as if it was something I had been waiting for. Now, all of a sudden, I have to decide what's important and what isn't, what in this world I no longer want to deal with, and what I absolutely must do.

Even the slenderest event assumed a fateful dimension. The eve of my birthday found me rocking in my chair so hard that it keeled over. Clearly, this was blind fate protecting me from the trip I was planning the following day.

Time, death, and myself … any distraction from all this came in very handy. You clean out the drains, wash the curtains, sew new ones, have trouble shortening the metal rod without a hacksaw to hand. You take lascivious delight in tidying up and cleaning the flat. Better leave washing the windows for tougher times. You at last let your innate propensity for DIY have its head. You are familiar with all the hygiene-related fuss from that time in Odessa, the only task that's new is the sewing of protective masks.[1] Even white gloves are to hand: ten pairs that I inherited from my mother. I discover exemplary reserves in the pantry, having done a lot of cooking, though little eating. On my balcony, to the odds and ends of the greenery that had survived the winter in the flower boxes I added yellow calendula, salad greens, chives, sprouting onions, garlic, and herbs. At night I went to bed with the self-deceiving feeling of work well done.

I had no idea of the impending collapse of the socialist regime in 1989, but I can say with absolute certainty that, as far as the coming of this particular turning-point was concerned, I could feel it in my bones and was quite ready for it.

---

1   Zsuzsa Hetényi, "'Chorela' Quarantine (Odessa, 1975)," *Los Angeles Review of Books*, April 10, 2020: http://lareviewofbooks.org/article/chorela-quarantine-odessa-1975/

Though I didn't know what exactly was coming; I just suspected it was approaching. Pressure has piled upon pressure worldwide. Conflicts have accumulated. Already folk were travelling far too much, the sheeplike crowds corralled into barnlike shelters at the airport, especially on the shabbier flight routes. I started to prefer to take the train. I tried not to travel too far and never for short trips. I would rather go less often and stay longer each time. The crowds, overwhelming the exotic landscapes, seething and foaming as they made their presence all too felt as they liberally flashed about with their selfies, I already found alarming. At conferences and book launches I surveyed those present with compassion, asking myself why they weren't allowed to stay home and write in peace, the way I longed to myself. I felt a pained sympathy for the Danube because I felt sorry for all its wasted water; I felt bad about the ever-shrinking distant rainforests. Being a health- and pocket-conscious shopper didn't make me too popular, nor did my role either as a representative of the blue-and-yellow recycling bin movement, or as a pilgrim prepared to wander a long way with my empty bottles. I have no problem saying no to heavily advertised branded goods and vastly overpriced foods. I am constantly shocked by the fever of self-indulgent panic buying.

Shortages leave me cold: self-restraint is a natural concomitant of survival. I'm not sermonizing to others, just tipping my hat to my parents. It's not only the shoes that make holes in the socks, but our own heels rub against them too. It's unfortunate that only those who have already felt a stinging pain somewhere can be aware of the movement of all their muscles while walking. This applies to all our environmental issues. If the entire population of China enjoyed America's standard of living, we would need two more planets like the Earth to keep them alive.

To me the powerful new wave of the literature of memory and life-writing suggests that we're just putting our old world into a museum for a future that is both terrifying and unknown. Because there is something that's just about to disappear forever. This is confirmed by the fact that there is now a massive new wave of Holocaust remembrance, a burgeoning of Facebook groups focused on collecting old photos, retro objects and the popular art of the very recent past.

Foreign colleagues, whom I met only at conferences, deluged me with letters of condolence when news reached them of the Hungarian government's measures undermining democracy and looking after their own, who are already better off. Only the previous week the faceless virus was on the prowl: now the face of someone running amok came out into the open, its maskless mouth spewing lie after lie.

The more information I have, the less I know. This also applies to the virus, which can consume the entire body. What really terrifies me, however, is the revelation that the professionals are playing no part in decision-making. Chaos, impetuosity, vulnerability, where there should be trust, solidarity, compassion. Has the economy really collapsed? Can human life really be without worth? Must one really choose between these two: isn't there some more sensible solution? Can a country's government really change its position overnight? Pontius Pilate has been disinfecting his hands in vain for two thousand years. Those hurrying to save their skins and power will not sound the ambulance's siren. Stubborn leaders, sunken in vulgar aggression in their insecurity, have a shaky hold even on their mother tongue … It's no accident that the dictators' chief enemies are healthcare and education – everything essential to preserve the human condition.

In week three of the pandemic, I received a request from a Russian researcher asking for a good Russian translation of an Endre Ady poem, but I couldn't find one. While fiddling around doing a rough translation, all of a sudden, I realized that it was one I had already struggled with in high school just for my own pleasure. I dug out my old exercise books, but I couldn't find the notes anywhere. I also took out my old diaries, which I didn't open even during the renovations, while packing and unpacking. Now I read them, in amazement. Some of the pages I had stuck together when my children were born, and now I cursed my former self, because instead of depriving my descendants of my secrets, it was myself that I had deprived of them. Memories came flooding back. My adolescent self took me back to memories of my mother and father. I kept pulling out old documents, going back to my grandparents and even beyond. I tried to make some sense of those old letters and photographs. I spent days downloading documents from old Hungarian newspapers freely released during the first phase of the virus. The news of my grandfather's brother's death cropped up while I was collecting my mother's articles from the sixties, a photo of myself in a pioneer's red bandana surfaced. Time stood still, I was staying up late, getting up late. Easter and birthdays slipped by unnoticed, spring break was skipped, as we used it to prepare our materials for distance learning, and only the rhythm of the remote classes held time together. News about cultural programs we were supposed to read and listen to came pouring in, but personally I didn't watch a single movie or play. The movies and performances that were good in the past I could remember well, and what had been boring then remained just as boring now. The intoxication of music assisted with the intoxication of writing and reading, though not now the usual kind of music: the organ, Pink Floyd, Erik Satie, rather, to go with the retro feel of vinyl and tape.

What will change? (2)

The most unexpected consequence – Cov-sequence? – will be that the generations will grow further apart. That's not something I'm hearing from other countries at the moment. It's in the interests of the younger, Y and Z generations, that those ready to retire should free up their jobs, yet Generation X, in mid-career and not intending to retire for another twenty years, are at the forefront of sounding the retreat for the older folk.

I fear that communities that survive the crisis will not be able to come together. In the course of just a single day in April I witnessed the disintegration of an editorial board, an association, a club, and a family. The successive collapse of long-term friendships, of desires and plans among workgroups and communities, the first warning lights of failure, strangle such attempts at birth.

Much has already been said about the twentieth century but looking back from the moment of the first wave of the pandemic I suddenly understood that it had been a century of lies. The concept of the short twentieth century – between

1914 and 1991– as argued by Eric Hobsbawm was immediately overwritten for me by that of the long twentieth century of lies, which has just now come to an end.

While as responsible civil servants we switched from face-to-face university education to distance learning during the spring break, I like many others immersed myself in the floodtide of news, only to realize the very next day – or even the same day – the half- and skewed truths and lies based on fake data that lay concealed behind it all. The manufacturing of secrets, the encrypting of data, is also a form of lying; the withholding of information is power. It was a lie that started the epidemic, but that was not the only reason that made me – and many others – immediately recall Chernobyl: it was the fact that in April 1986, too, spring was in full, inviting bloom, and we watched from behind closed windows how death invisible stalked the land. Lettuce, milk, nature itself – the earth itself – became enemies. Common enemies.

The virus, too, is invisible. It's harder to visualize. It has no cells, yet it devours, living a parasitical existence, and no one knows how it chooses its victims. We are only just beginning to understand the way it kills. Even if it is a common enemy, the knowledge that it can be given to us by the "Other" atomizes society, forcing states to barricade within their borders. Few are capable of radiating love from a distance of two meters, or from a screen.

The use of the blue-yellow recycling bins is just one example. Those who don't think through where the waste will go when it is thrown away, and where else, if not there, will only get used to it like an automaton, or for fear of punishment (Switzerland). The yellow-blue-trash rite may seem ridiculous to others. Perhaps it's self-deception. I'm not interested in skeptical voices that claim "everything will end up in the same heap anyway". Anyway, anyway... we will all die anyway. I'm talking about what is our own business, ourselves, about looking in the mirror and (seeing) reflections. Because *I, too, am part of the environment*, that is, my body, my own body, is in need of care and protection. From now on, I won't wear uncomfortable clothes or go to boring events, or visit people who bore me, out of mere politeness.

Ritual is the basis of environmental protection and health care. It's nothing more than knowing why we do what we do. We endow it with meaning, meaningfulness, and that's why we keep repeating things in the same way. Eventually, it will become the building block of our own selves. In order to develop the ritual, we shift to an associative (symbolic, analytical) way of thinking. Dictatorships are poor at tolerating thinking people.

The person or team that allowed the virus to escape from the market or from the lab, or let those initially infected leave hospital, was incapable of thinking through where the virus might end up. Or if they were, they were criminals. This narrative is reinforced by the silencing those who warned of the danger. But equally scary is the epidemic of criminal or unfit leaders in power. Hazardous waste themselves, they too will end up on the vast trash heap of the universe. Environmental protection is also nature's self-defense.

In one of Nabokov's novels, *Transparent Things*, the protagonist finds an old pencil in his hotel room. The thread of the narrative stops, and an entire chapter is devoted to where the pencil came from, where its wood was cut, how the timber was floated downriver, and where and how its graphite was compressed. I am likewise reminded of the Danube when I collect the water runoff for irrigation when I just switch between cold and hot water. I do it not to save money myself because my water is not metered.

Evil fate (McFate) has now ensured that everyone musts follow a set of rituals. Now everyone practice separation. This shoe for outside wear, that one for indoors. That dress outdoors, this one at home. This mask is already dirty, that one's clean. Do I take it off outside or indoors? Wearing gloves or not? Before or after washing hands? How do I take off my possibly infectious gloves? How many meters' distance do I keep when talking to my neighbor? How many days does the virus remain infectious on any particular material? On paper just one day, otherwise seven?

Relying on rituals provides reassurance. Perhaps we can turn the ritual into routine. I'm sure my age-group will be quarantined for several more months. We'll see what will remain to remind us of our life before the epidemic's fall, and what will disappear. I have no knowledge, only intuitions.

What can give us hope, what can we rely on? (3)

On ourselves, on analogies, on the written word, on human gestures. It so happened that in the course of my life I've had to sum up several times what I could depend on.

"O you who share with me this age! don't turn to your doctors, don't turn to the priests, when you find yourselves inwardly." Hölderlin's precise message from the past is quoted by someone, in someone else's translation. These intermediaries, plus the author, represent three ages, and our acknowledgment of them connects us all through space and time. One, as an intellectual, a literary scholar, a translator, and a professor (depending in which role I imagine and feel myself to be at a given moment) is constantly reflecting on something and constantly looking for points of reference. Default setting. Normal mode. It cannot be ruled out that the Hungarians' immune system is strengthened by a strong literature, in addition to vaccination.

The concept of the author I most often cite, Vladimir Nabokov, that death is not a fading away but back into the cosmos and nature, is of little help these days, unless as faith-like self-deception. A great disadvantage of the current disease and of many other forms of death is that death is preceded not only by suffering, but also by the humiliating nature of Hungary's horrendous hospital and social conditions. Probably this is much scarier and lasts longer than death itself. So this is not the ecstatic poetry of melding back into nature that Russian poets imagine. The sarcasm of Nabokov is far more useful. "The folly of chance is the logic of fate." Now, that is universal – if somewhat half-empty/half-full, both discouraging and encouraging.

Close to my way of thinking is what Nabokov calls cosmic synchronization. This has been over-inflated by philosophically inclined analysts. It means that one can embrace and feel simultaneously several events at several distant points in the world. If one gives it free associative rein, there will be an increase in its emotional appeal, at least in peacetime. Even if not with cosmic, but with all-earth-embracing eyes we now look at the virus world map, we can see, in addition to disfig-ured nature and millions living in dirt, we can see crowded hospital corridors, wheezing patients, exhausted doctors, sobbing relatives, desperate fates. A Hun-garian periphery is also taking shape, with communities without work, education, housing, and food. It causes us physical pain because mere compassion will not do. Helpless rage, or rather, rage induced by helplessness, is directed at all those irresponsible and ineffective people unable to do their job properly. I am living and growing old in a chaotic state where lack of expertise is disguised by arro-gant confidence. Donations, petitions, protests do little about remorse. Instead of self-reproach we need self-approach, a U-turn.

The opposite of the cosmic wide-angle lens, yet its brother, is the close-up. Leaning down close and deep, the discovery of shapes and patterns is just as great a discovery, providing no less joy. The revelation of ordered beauty in something tiny is profoundly comforting. Close-ups of nature, of phenomena, of objects. In the slowdown of the lockdown sitting at home opened the eyes of others to this, too, so it is no longer just "a most rare variety of madness" (as Nabokov put it) of mine to photograph the fractal rose of a split cabbage, to revel in the still of the snap. Millions of folk can share the fascinating view from their kitchen of a crumbling, ivy-clad firewall, and what a curious, filtered light a glass of tea casts on the table. The all-but-forbidden, liberating walks, too, now reveal Nature with a capital N as a miracle for those who have so far been going to the gym in search of strength, health, and friends there.

Russian literature and history can be applied so directly to the situation today that it should be available on prescription. If hospitals are being emptied simply to secure a certain number of beds for the COVID sick, Gogol's novel *Dead Souls* is recommended: in it wealth and rank can be gathered from the dead. Apparent wealth. And only for a time. I teach Stalinism every semester, so when a hospital director was dismissed for not emptying the buildings of elderly patients within forty-eight hours, it immediately occurred to me that they could also have had him shot. For failing to implement the five-year plan in two days.

I am reminded of the danger of death by Cincinnatus in Nabokov's *Invitation to a Beheading*: he is informed of his death sentence in a completely absurd, petty operetta dictatorship, and then he is merely left to shrivel in prison. But one of Cincinnatus's selves survives solely because he begins to write a prison (quarantine) diary. The subject of the diary is himself, because "no one can take me away from myself". Loneliness is the fundamental form of human existence.

Soviet reality is also a good school for practicing distancing oneself from the contagion and filth of the outside world, but about death and lies the toughest reckoning for me is still provided by Samuel Beckett's essay on Proust. We cannot bend the future to our will because it collapses all by itself, and (or because?) the world must be recreated, again and again, every single day. "Whatever opinion we may be pleased to hold on the subject of death, we may be sure that it is meaningless and valueless." What is meaningless, our opinion or the death?

Anything can be compared to anything; comparisons can only be beneficial. Comparing literature to life is so easy that it is already smacks of bad taste. Sergei Dovlatov, who I am teaching this week, emigrated with a single suitcase. At first, he thought that the three suitcases he was allowed to take were insufficient, but in the end, he realized that just one was quite enough. Even in that single one he put only inessential memorabilia. Even after his arrival, he didn't open it for years, but then wrote a novel in America, each chapter being the story of one of the objects in it. I wonder what I would take with me in my suitcase if Noah's ark or Charon's boat came for me … It would take too much time thinking about it: it would probably be easier to torch everything. It was in that spirit that I filled a hospital bag in readiness.

The genetic experience of the gas chamber's shadow is also a wake-up slap on the cheek. What a privilege it is to be able to prepare for death in relatively good health, not starving, and not in animal-like humiliation. Likewise, however, you should follow the concentration camp principle and only look as far ahead as the next step, the next day.

The emblem of survival is the mask. I have everything for sewing masks here at home: old linen shirts, strips from bedsheets, thick kitchen towels waiting to be cut up, ribbon, rubber, cord, rope, string, yarn, even shoelaces – and a sewing machine. I had fun playing with the designs for a while, then made ten or more, all different, the neatest for my younger son.

Then two world-renowned patents popped out of my head. You can turn upside down the eye masks used on flights and pull them down to cover nose and mouth. I had seven of those at home, one for each day of the week, so that the virus could die its death on it. Or you cut the short sleeve off a tired T-shirt. Take some knicker elastic long enough to wrap around your head twice and tie the ends together. Ribbon (or elastic, cord, rope, string, yarn, even shoelaces) will do, but then make it a little longer for the bow. Put the rope around your neck – on this occasion with peaceful intent – draw the tee-shirt sleeve over it and place the protruding loop ends over your ears. Soon the only thing giving you a headache will be which mask to put on when. When I'm going out. But I'm not going out. The masks pile up for posterity's Museum of Masks.

What's your coping strategy? (+1 = 4)

Making choices in everything carefully. Separating things is an ancient biblical injunction. That was how the creation of the world took place: by separating things.

There remain the old rituals and routines, since anyone who has found work the best way of passing the time has, in any case, spent most of their time alone. What remains? Really good friends, the joys of keeping house, morning exercises, daily walks, weekly escapes to the mountains, hills, and forests. Free association — when I'm just thinking about what I'm thinking. It's a very interesting way of becoming acquainted with what's in my mind. As I am inundated by memories, they become broader and sharper.

This may well be an individual strategy. Rather than in the community, I now tend to trust more in the relationship between two people, face to face, mind to mind. The way the arcane doctrines were passed on.

With my tender teenage lover, we had a quotation from the Bible that we found together, which we rendered in our own translation: "You may do anything, but not everything will edify you."

Small-time Scammers
An Excerpt from *Victory Park*

Alexei Nikitin

Translated from the Russian
by Catherine O'Neil

1

Vilya woke up slowly, heavily disentangling himself from a foggy pre-dawn night-mare – then he sat up quickly and tossed off the blanket. The room was quiet and dark. He couldn't remember his dream and he didn't understand where he was. Vilya was seeing the room he'd just spent the night for the first time: a bulky, pol-ished wardrobe, some trash piled up, a TV on a side table – an "Elektron," appar-ently – a cheap rug on the floor, clothing hooks, and shelves on the walls. On the rug he saw his shoes, jeans and hastily discarded women's underwear. The room smelled of dust and unwashed clothes. It smelled like an unloved and neglected space, a place where people don't live but drop in, without pleasure and without the loving attention to the small things that make life, if not exactly meaningful, then at least help camouflage its dreary facelessness. And Vilya loved the small things. He was a master of detail.

"Misha," a sleepy voice drifted over from behind him. "Are you up already?"

Misha…. Oh, right. Of course. Vilya looked around carefully. A slightly plump knee and round woman's hand peeked out from under the blanket. The right hand, judging from the wedding ring on it. Vilya pensively stroked the knee: what was her name again?

"Yes, darling. And I really need some coffee."

"Then make me some too. The coffee is in the tin on the counter by the stove…."

Vilya had hoped to hear slightly different words than these but wasn't about to argue.

"Of course, sunshine." His hand made its leisurely way along the smooth skin of a feminine hip and disappeared beneath the blanket. From under the pillow contented rumbling could be heard.

"Make some coffee and hurry back, darling."

Now she'll tell all her friends that Misha Boyarsky brought her coffee in bed. Vilya grinned.

Getting up from the bed, he quickly pulled on his worn old Levi's and, looking for his shirt, glanced around the room once more. Vilya had bought the jeans last summer. He took two pairs for eighty rubles from the Finn from the Leninsky Ship Factory at the hard currency bar in the "Lybid" hotel. He passed the second pair off to Belfast for a hundred, more than regaining his loss. Then Belfast resold them for two hundred at the "point." Vilya wasn't a full-time *fartsovshchik*, just occasionally made some black market deals when he ran into foreigners. But for Belfast this business was a carefully staged operation.

Vilya found his Wrangler shirt on the floor, in the corner between the wall and the wardrobe. Bunched into a tight heap, it lay piled in the dust under the mirror.

Ever since childhood Vilya had hated mirrors, particularly in the dimness of dark and empty apartments. He was afraid of water, darkness, and mirrors. When he grew older, Vilya learned to manage his relationship with mirrors if he was in the glare of well-lit halls and studios, but even now he instinctively recoiled from the darkness reflected by glass. He could return to the devilish mirror afterwards and, getting a grip on himself, could even look into it. But his initial reaction remained unchanged.

Buttoning up his shirt, Vilya stepped out from behind the wardrobe and, gathering all his courage, tried to examine his reflection. In the dimly lit bedroom you could only discern his luxurious "Boyarsky" mustache, distinctively darkening his still untanned face.

In the next room the ruins of their late-night supper awaited him. Hardened bread, wilting greens and wrinkled cucumbers sat sorrowfully next to dried-out tomatoes. A large fly rose up from the Finnish sausage, heavy and lazy, and cut a circle above the table before landing on the remains of some herring. An empty bottle of whiskey lay on the floor by the balcony doors. The cognac and candies were gone from the table; no doubt, Belfast and Aphrodita's friend had taken them on their way out.

Aphrodita! That was the name of the drowsy owner of the plump knee and wedding ring who awaited her morning coffee on the other side of the wall.

Vilya cut off a slice of sausage, then another, spiked an olive from the salad with a fork and went into the kitchen.

Belfast had brought him to this apartment the night before. At 6 PM, after work, Vilya had closed up the photo studio in Shevchenko Park and headed down the boulevard toward Kreshchatik Street. Lilac trees were blooming in full force, warming the park itself as well as the surrounding courtyards with their thick, sweet aroma. The girls in the black and white portraits hanging in the studio window shone barely perceptible smiles at Vilya, at each other, and at everyone else who found themselves in the park that early evening. Freshness was already drifting in from the Botanical Gardens. Swifts soared up high, above the brown rooftops of buildings lit up by the sun setting in the west, calling out to each other as they circled. It was May, the way May can only be in Kiev.

Vilya walked with a light step. He hadn't decided yet how to spend the evening that lay before him in all its splendor. There was a pair of Puma sneakers in the leather bag thrown over his shoulder – 36's, the size most popular with women. During his lunch break he had made the rounds of his usual addresses: the Theater Hotel and the Intourist on Lenin Street, the Leningrad and Ukraine Hotels on Shevchenko Boulevard. At the Ukraine Hotel he got lucky: the fourth-floor attendant, Ninochka, brought him to the room of a West German *bundes* and the tourist sold him the sneakers for just fifty. Belfast, Harley or Alabama would give Vilya at least a hundred for them without thinking twice, but if he took his time and looked for a buyer himself, then he might even get a hundred seventy for the new red and white Pumas.

Turning onto Bessarabka, Vilya paused for a minute, considering which way he should head that evening. Kreshchatik beckoned him with a burst of sunlight in the windows of its upper floors. Deciding this was a sign, Vilya quickly crossed the street by the underground passage and emerged under the chestnut trees on the odd-numbered side of the street. Some female university students and thirty-year-old femme fatales (the kind the streets of Kiev produced in abundance) followed him with their eyes – as did their jealous companions, guys who had prematurely gotten heavy on rich borscht and "lazy" dumplings. Everyone looked at him as he passed. Vilya was wearing Italian sunglasses, as though hiding behind their dark lenses from intolerably curious glances. But in fact, as he knew perfectly well, his resemblance to the Soviet Union's first musketeer was only heightened when he wore those glasses.

"It's Boyarsky! Look, Boyarsky!" The Kiev beauties got weak in their knees. "My God, it's really him!"

Vilya strode along the Kreshchatik asphalt as though it were the red carpet and he was on his way to receive a recent and well-earned Oscar; no time to stop and smile at the cameras and give autographs to his fans, woozy from excitement.

Kreshchatik, however, was not merely a place for leisurely strolls arm in arm with your girl, flowing with vanilla ice-cream in waffle cones on sale for nineteen kopecks apiece. For many it was a boiler room, a work pit, a smithy – in other words, a web of "points." Vilya typically passed the first "point" – next to the entrance to the underground passage – without stopping, like a trolleybus heading back to the depot. Everything was too visible, there was too much activity – it was almost impossible to hide from unwanted and curious eyes. The second, on the other hand, next to the "Michigan" bar – could not be dismissed so easily. As soon as he passed the shop "Bulgarian Rose," Vilya spotted a familiar figure. Venya "minus-seven-diopters" was blinking his eyes so trustingly at the swifts in the Kiev sky that the casual buyer would never have suspected in this lanky and infantile fellow the most experienced *fartsovshchik* on the Krest. He had been stopped a dozen times but for some reason was always released. Who knows, maybe it really was just the way that Venya would bat his eyelashes and helplessly stare, moving up close to the eyes of Lieutenant Zhitny, that eternal boy with the balding head in a policeman's cap.

"What's that? What am I selling on the black market today? Sorry, but I can hardly see anything. I am legally blind. I have a doctor's certificate, do you want to see it?"

"Yeah, I know, I know." Zhitny waved his hand dismissively. "You have bad vision, citizen Sokol, but you hear just fine."

Venya Sokol could both hear and see perfectly, much better than Lieutenant Zhitny. Six years ago he had left the Russian Dramatic Theater, abandoned the stage altogether, and chosen the career of *fartsovshchik*. And he had never looked back. He could see his home theater from his "point" any time and any day he wanted; if he ever had the urge to see any of their performances an aisle seat in the orchestra section was always set aside for him. But Venya despised the Russian Dramatic Theater and only deigned to accept his aisle seat when the Moscow or Georgian companies toured. He had seen Sturuya's production of Brecht's *Caucasian Chalk Circle* exactly as many times as the Tbilisi actors had performed it.

This morning, by the church, I told Georgi Abashvili that I love a clear sky. But really I love a storm within a clear sky even more, yes indeed.

The Georgian actors, no strangers to the glamor of either Tbilisi or Moscow, remembered for a long time after the handsome, elegant gentleman from Kiev who at their farewell banquet presented each man a bottle of Irish whiskey and each woman a set of French lingerie. What's more, the lingerie fit each actress, without exception, astonishingly well.

If by some implausible, capricious chance his policeman's fate had suddenly landed Lieutenant Zhitny at that banquet, he would never have recognized the half-blind and hush-voiced Venya "Minus-seven-diopters."

But Vilya was not destined to chat with Venya that day. He walked by the fabric store and the first gentle drops of the fountain (installed by caring city authorities in front of the "Michigan") exploded with sunlight before landing on the polarized Italian lenses of Vilya's sunglasses. Just then a short, portly, completely bald man hurriedly crossed his path.

"You are on the right path, Comrade!" theatrically bellowed the short, bald man who embraced Vilya as if he hadn't seen him for years. "And that path leads to me."

"Hello there, Belfast!" Vilya thought about the sneakers in his bag and decided not to mention them for now.

"You are free today, I trust?" Belfast took Vilya's arm and pulled him nearer. "The evening has just begun – and though the stars have not yet appeared in our southern skies we have been promised a romantic night. Are you ready?"

In fact, there was little tempting in Belfast's proposal. Vilya knew perfectly well that his "romantic night" was nothing more than the umpteenth drinking party with some vile females from the main trade office in the Gorispolkom. Or from the Kiev Food Commission, Kievlegpishchesnabsbyt. Or from the UkrPrec-Metals trade commission. Or from the UkrForCurr trade commission. It was especially for these ageing, oversexed bitches that countless departments, trusts, and offices had been established. Along the silt-clogged bureaucratic canals sunk into the semi-desert of a socialist governance that weakened year by year, but never quite dried up, flowed foreign goods and the oscillating national deficit. The pudgy hands of the women civil servants masterfully opened or closed the necessary sluice gates so that some fields sprouted and grew green while others dried up and the harvest failed.

Oh, how inaccessible they were in their offices decorated with trademark varnished furniture and the requisite profile of the leader on one wall and the general secretary facing him on the other! How disdainfully they would look at their visitor through lowered eyelashes! How well they could smile, conveying with a barely noticeable movement of their painted lips the exact degree of their bureaucratic haughtiness and fastidious indifference.

Belfast found all these unassailable bastions amusing. He knew how to conquer them, where to find the chinks in their bureaucratic armor, invisible at first glance. And even the ones who already had everything, who only ate from the hand of a single master and furiously barked at strangers, paying no heed to hints and tempting treats – even these he could conquer with a single name: Boyarsky. Boyarsky! The cold eyes of these officious bitches would immediately brighten with new life. And in their smiles appeared, not exactly a trusting attentiveness, but at least some readiness to listen further, to go somewhere, to meet somewhere beyond the walls of this varnished office. A readiness to remove their armor and replace it with the charming Italian outfit that they had had no occasion to wear until now.

"But is Misha really in Kiev?"

"He is, but only for two days. And only one evening – then he flies home. He's been invited to the studio to discuss his new film."

"How wonderful, Misha in Kiev! Maybe he'll sing something?"

"Let us not forget that Misha is an actor, a creative personality. Maybe he'll sing something, and maybe he won't."

Ah, the unpredictability of actors! Ah, their tantalizing lack of commitment, their ability to so pleasantly shake up the dreariness of everyday life in which everything has been ordered, scheduled and determined long ago once and for all: you may do this, you may not do that, and under no circumstances should you do that. To sing with Boyarsky! To sing his most famous song: "A-ap! I have even tamed tigers…". To sing, your hand placed on his shoulder, imbibing the scent of his French *eau de cologne* – I mean, he's not going to smell of Soviet "Chipre" after all.

Belfast smiled mysteriously, not promising anything; in this absence of promise much more could be hidden then if he had offered all at once both the songs from "The Three Musketeers" and dancing with Misha to the beat of Arabesque.

In fact, everything had been pre-arranged with Vilya long in advance – and tested more than once. Vilya would show up late, arriving about an hour and a half after the appointed time, when the bureaucrat ladies, slightly fatigued from anticipation, had already had a shot of vodka each and sampled a morsel of the most tender sturgeon, obtained by Belfast from the womb of UkrMainRivFleet. They'd usually even repeated the process and moved on to the caviar.

Vilya would burst like a fresh breeze into their musty parlors of the best decor, with chiffon and velvet on the windows and plush corduroy sofas. He would laugh a white-toothed laugh, still on the move, toss back a drink, kiss all the ladies' hands. He'd tell the latest amusing anecdote, drink another shot of vodka and, laughing again, quickly summarize the latest gossip from *Piter* – all before sitting down. Then he would apologize, embrace Belfast and complain that he would be called away at any moment to the theater, the recording, the filming. That the taxi to the airport was waiting for him all this time in the front driveway. It was true: a checkered "Volga" could be seen from the window, a yellow light on the upper right side of the windshield flashing reproachfully and insistently.

"At least take a photo with us, Misha! A photo as a souvenir!"

And Misha – that is, Vilya – would not refuse. Before dashing off into the beautiful realm beyond the clouds he would obediently sit down on the plush sofa, in the very center of the overripe bouquet of Italian outfits. Vilya smiled his white-toothed smile, delicately squeezing the flabby sides of his neighbors, feeling their soft, tender fingers adorned with cold diamond rings against his neck, and their breath – smelling of vodka, fish, and the traces of the unsuccessful work of our national dentists – against his cheeks.

"Sing for us, Misha! Sing before you go, eh? Sing 'Aaap!…'!" The ladies would get presumptuous and cross the line of what was permitted. "Look, we even have a guitar!"

And Vilya would smile at them affectionately, if a little reproachfully, as if to say: don't forget, my dears, who it is before you and where the trumpets of glory are beckoning him. There was not a trace of coarse vanity or cutting arrogance in his smile, which the ladies there would have recognized immediately. That was something they understood better than anyone else. No, there was only regret at the impossibility of staying longer in this charming company and a slight fatigue from the hurried and constantly moving life he was obliged to lead.

Vilya would have even sung something if he could. He would definitely have sung; Belfast would have found enough arguments and reasons for him. But Vilya's talents only went as far as his outward qualities. The mustachioed photographer from Shevchenko Park had a tin ear.

Misha would take his leave, the taxi would tear off from its spot and drive off into the night, and Belfast would stay on with the amused and relaxed ladies, who would endlessly thank him for those minutes of rare happiness. And the fact that Misha hadn't sung only worked to Belfast's advantage. It meant there was still something for them to wish for in life, it meant Boyarsky would sing for them the next time. He would certainly sing, no way around it. Both "Aaap!" and "City Flowers." It meant they would feel joy once again in their life, and it meant that they would need Belfast again some time. That useful man with his remarkable friend.

Except these evening masquerades didn't thrill his friend Vilya that much. Obviously, if the trick were ever exposed, what then? No, they weren't con artists and hadn't extorted any money from these high-placed ladies. No one could prove any mercenary motives in their behavior. Vilya for sure had none. But every time he imagined the potential vengeance of these deceived women Vilya would freeze in horror: their innocent amusements could end very unpleasantly indeed. And what did Belfast care? He would worm his way out no matter what. He would just say: I didn't know either, that mustached rogue took me in. Vilya would be left to dig his way out on his own.

"You know, old friend," Vilya carefully liberated his arm from Belfast's and sat down on a bench beneath a chestnut tree. Belfast sat down next to him. "These performances for the assistants to trade union bosses have worn me out. Let's finish with all this Boyarism. Let's just be ourselves for a bit."

"Vilya, I understand you better than anyone." Belfast put a fatherly hand on his shoulder. "You know I rarely ask you to do anything for me. Only for business. But today is a completely different situation. Maybe for the first time I need you to do this for me. Hmm? As a friend. I've already told them that I'd bring Boyarsky. The silly cows didn't believe me. Well, we'll show them…"

"Who is 'them'?" Vilya sighed. He already saw he couldn't get out of it this time either.

"She'll have a friend with her. Come on, why not? It'll be more fun."

So Vilya agreed to go.

They headed for the Bessarabsky Market to get some herring and vegetables to add to the bottle of whiskey, Finnish sausage, and the jar of black caviar already lying in Belfast's briefcase – all to adorn the evening for two busy people of liberal views and professions. Vilya had barely had time to ask the price of some Crimean apricots when Belfast, waving to someone, firmly grabbed his arm and steered him toward the market's health inspection office. Quickly trotting on short legs, a small man with a mustache in a white apron brought over a pineapple and a bunch of bananas. Belfast fastidiously prodded the fruit with two fingers and gave a slight nod. Then another man came in, exactly as mustached and short-legged as the first, bringing Belfast a bottle of Napoleon brandy, Crimean sparkling wine, and a box of "Evening Kiev" chocolates.

Ten minutes later, Belfast's car, a Lada "Eight," was already turning from Kirov Street to Petrovsky Alley in order to cross the Metro Bridge; it drove past Hydropark and proceeded along the Left Bank Highway, and then turned onto Komsomolsky Massif. It came to a stop next to a bloc of twelve-story high-rises, assembled in a semi-circle.

"We're practically at my house." Vilya looked around as he got out of the car. "Victory Park is right over there – I used to be a *fartsovshchik* here, working for Alabama. There's the Darnitsa metro station. It's not even twenty minutes to my place from here, or five minutes on wheels. And School 204 is next door. Belfast, I graduated from that school seven years ago and, they tell me, I haven't changed a bit since. Except that back then I didn't have a mustache. Every slut in the Massif knows me. I'll say it again: it's not worth me playing Boyarsky around here."

"Vilya, calm down." Belfast clapped him on the shoulder and, taking an armful of their purchases, headed for the door. "Let's hurry up or the girls will cool off. And forget your panic. She is from Lithuania, her name is Aphrodita. She doesn't know anyone here and, although she may have her doubts, she believes in miracles and is waiting for Boyarsky to visit – like all of them. So let's give her a miracle, since it's so easy to do."

Belfast, it turned out, was right – indeed, he always was. The slight doubt lurking behind the initial polite smiles from Aphrodita and her older friend Elena dispersed instantly as soon as the pineapple and bananas were laid out on the table in the living room. A bottle of scotch was placed next to the "Napoleon," the product of Finnish sausage-makers and the black caviar. Not once since the day of its creation had this table seen items of such fabulous luxury on its surface at the same time. And if their guest's complete physical resemblance to their favorite actor had for some reason not convinced the wary ladies, then his gifts spoke for themselves and for him. Who else could produce all this in a tiny Kiev apartment on the very edge of the city, at the edge of the forest?

"Girls!" Belfast commanded in a decisive tone. "Let's cut some sandwiches and the herring, and get out whatever salads you may have on hand. Although we are almost unexpected guests I am sure that you have a few salads already prepared. Misha has some time – and definitely time for you – but not much. A taxi has already been ordered for ten o'clock to take him to Borispol Airport, and tomorrow our honored Russian artist is awaited in the Lensoviet Theater. Besides, the artist is hungry. He's spent the whole day with administrative snouts in the Dovzhenko studio. So let's get started! Time is working against us, but you know what we have on our side? What we have on our side is – love!"

Belfast was a smart and successful man, but he didn't always sense the differ-ence between appropriate pathos and inappropriate vulgarity. Maybe it was for this very reason – that he didn't get bogged down in petty details – that Belfast was such a success.

"Ditka!" Aphrodita's friend Lena sprang into the kitchen after Belfast's little speech, her wonderstruck eyes barely fitting on her round, Ukrainian face. "It's the real Boyarsky! And to think I didn't believe you, what an idiot!"

"Mmhmm…" Aphrodita absentmindedly nodded, not pausing in her quick chopping of the cucumbers. "I had my doubts too. Get me the boiled eggs from the fridge. And the jar of mayonnaise."

Leaving the table in the ladies' hands, Vilya and Belfast stepped out onto the balcony. Beneath them was a green Kiev courtyard, not yet burnt out or withered yellow under the blazing summer sun. In the shade of sixteen-story towers apri-cots and cherries peacefully ripened, children shouted something, building care-takers hosed down the asphalt.

"What do you think?" Belfast asked, getting a pack of Moscow "Java" ciga-rettes from his pocket.

"Aphrodita is certainly pretty," Vilya smiled, looking over the familiar courtyard. "But Lena is a real beauty – although it's obvious she's not exactly twenty any more. But to tell the truth, I've always been afraid of women like her. I'm sure she hangs her husband up on a hook in the closet. She takes him down when she wants, and then sends him back to the mothballs. But lots of men chase after her type."

"Fine," Belfast laughed. "You just work for a couple of hours and I'll take over from there. I really owe you, Vilya."

"It's fine," Vilya waved him off.

Everything that evening might have followed the usual program, worked out months before, were it not for the unofficial status of the meeting. Not burdened by his typical sense of responsibility, Vilya relaxed. After the two scripted glasses of whiskey he allowed himself a third. Then, with the tender herring and amazing salad prepared by Aphrodita's loving hands, he took a fourth. Both Aphrodita and her friend Lena (who, it turned out, was not from Kiev either, but had moved from Donetsk a few years ago and lived not far away, with her mother, daughter, and husband), somehow sat so cozily on either side of Vilya that his musketeer's arms of their own accord embraced both women firmly, not releasing either one or the other to Belfast, who sat sulking on his own in the corner. Had Vilya been ready at any moment to release Lena to his sorrowful friend, she herself wouldn't have gone. As for Dita – Vilya had no intention of releasing her anywhere, as she pressed her full, warm hip against him, smelling so subtly of sweet lilac from the Riga Dzintars factory. He quickly forgot that they had come here because Belfast had wanted to develop his recent acquaintance with Dita. The only thing that worried Vilya was forgetting that he was supposed to be Boyarsky.

Belfast, though slightly annoyed with Vilya, understood the delicacy of the situation and waited for ten o'clock to arrive. He patiently waited for the taxi to appear in which Vilya would leave – not for Borispol Airport, naturally, but to his own home or wherever he wanted to go, leaving Belfast alone with the girls. Then his time would arrive. The time of the true host of this celebration.

Who could have guessed that the swashbuckling, drunken musketeer Vilya would not hear a word about any taxi when it finally showed up and would categorically refuse to leave.

"I'm having such a good time with you girls," Vilya pouted at them in satisfaction, draining his whiskey and switching to the Napoleon brandy. "I refuse to go anywhere. I mean, why should I go to all these filming and recording sessions, the Lensoviet Theater, when I have you, such wonderful company!"

"Wow!" Lena jumped up and down exactly as if she'd just won a Moskvich car. "Misha's staying with us!"

Aphrodita didn't respond so passionately – her calm, Lithuanian temperament was clearly in evidence – but the grateful press of her hand communicated to Vilya how she received his decision.

"What are you talking about, Misha?" Belfast turned on Vilya with fury. "You have a plane to catch, or did you forget? A PLANE! To LENINGRAD! Let's get you out of here now! Or you'll be demoted so fast your head will spin. Once you were *honored*, now you're *a goner*." He remembered the old joke and got up to help Vilya extract himself from behind the table, get to the elevator and dissolve into the warm Kiev night.

"Don't you dare," Lena blocked Belfast's way with indignation. "Nice job breaking up a party! And no need to rush him, no one will demote Misha. If he were a captain, like some people" –Lena shot a look at Dita – "then maybe he could be demoted. But he's a musketeer! A musketeer can't be demoted!"

"He can only be killed," Belfast said, unexpectedly agreeing with her. His work had taught him to accept the softer blows of fate and only attempt to dodge the heavy ones. "So Misha will stay! Excellent! Then let's have a song. Sing for us, Misha!"

"Now that's more like it," Lena said in support of Belfast's idea. "Misha, sing us that song: 'A-ap! I have even tamed tigers…'!"

"Do we have a guitar here?" Belfast continued his subversive work. The taxi was still waiting in the driveway and he reckoned that if he could put pressure on him now, Vilya would run away after all, leaving him the field of this unexpected battle.

But though a guitar could not be found Vilya unexpectedly accepted the challenge.

"Let's sing!" He lurched to his feet from the sofa, but immediately swayed and, were it not for the shoulder caringly placed under him for support by Dita, Vilya may well have wound up on the floor. "Let's sing," he repeated, leaning his full weight on Aphrodita, "Only let's sing quietly. Really quietly. Like this: 'un-der the air-plane's wiiiing…'"

"The national artist is tired," Lena pronounced sadly. "What Leningrad? He's not in any shape to even leave the sofa."

"*Honored* artist," said Belfast with spite, correcting her. He wouldn't let Vilya forget this evening for a very long time. "What do you think, Lena? I'll let the taxi go then and I can take you home. It's late and I have my car."

"My place is close enough to walk," Lena shrugged. But she didn't refuse his offer.

They led Vilya to the next room and laid him out on the bed. Voices could be heard for some time longer in the living room; someone was making a phone call. Then the sound of the elevator could be heard and everything fell silent. Waiting a minute more, Vilya cracked open the door. The light in the living room was off but water was running in the kitchen. Dita was washing the dishes.

Vilya quietly walked up to her, embraced her from behind and, tickling her cheek with his mustache, whispered in her ear:

"I may not be a *national* artist but I play a decent drunk, don't you think?"

"Not bad," Aphrodita started in surprise but then laughed softly. And Vilya could finally detect in her voice the gentle Lithuanian accent he had been missing all evening. Aphrodita turned off the water, leaving the dishes unwashed, and faced Vilya. "But not that great either," she added. "I for one figured it out."

Pressing her to him more firmly, Vilya wanted to ask if she had figured anything else out, but decided not to test fate a second time. Today fate had been kind to him – and for now that was good enough.

2

The sun rose over the flat roofs of the construction site of the uncompleted department store "Children's World." It flooded the kitchen with bright light and no mercy, confirming Vilya's initial impression that the apartment's inhabitants didn't love their home – and in general got little joy from life, either because they didn't know how or they hadn't had the opportunity. Yet experience told him loudly and confidently that Aphrodita, half asleep in the next room, waiting for him to bring her morning coffee, was ready to take on a great deal to fill her life with joy; she was ready to fill it to the top, to dive into it as into a swimming pool caressed by the summer sun, forgetting everything else – and not afraid of the water brimming over. He doubted she'd be too upset to find out that her new acquaintance was not the Honored Artist of the Russian Soviet Republic at all, but an ordinary photographer from a studio in Shevchenko Park. What was Boyarsky to her, in the grand scheme? She maybe could have met up with the famous actor – if she naively supposed that they would meet up again – at most twice a year. But Vilya was right here, always by her side, always available. That is, of course, assuming she was available herself.

Vilya lit the burner for the Turkish coffee pot and cast a glance around the kitchen, looking for sugar. There wasn't any sugar. Vilya rummaged in the drawers, opened first one cupboard over the sink, then another – nothing. There wasn't any sugar in a third cupboard either, the one mounted on the opposite wall; it was clearly not intended for food but the meticulous Vilya checked it anyway. Instead, he found a policeman's cap.

"Well, well, our Dita's a cop." At first Vilya laughed, the idea didn't upset him in the least. It was a bit *piquant*, and the work of a playful fate could be seen in this development. He'd never had a woman in uniform before – this would be his first. But then another, more sobering thought followed. Vilya picked up the cap and saw that his first assumption had been wrong. There was no way Dita could wear a size 58 hat. This cap had to be worn by a man – and not a very clean man, judging by the sweat stained fabric on the band and the greasy spot where the cap touched the already balding crown of the man's head. A wedding ring, a police uniform in the house … all this demanded caution and careful consideration.

The untended apartment Belfast had brought him to the day before looked a lot like a cop's apartment. Not a pleasure-loving cop, a well-fed traffic cop or a lieutenant colonel who'd secured a comfortable sinecure in the republic's department of the interior. But a bloodhound cop, a fanatic, who spent fifteen hours a day at work and even in his sleep worked on unravelling criminal plots, unable to turn down any work trips and only remembering his home when the cleaning lady came in to tidy his office. Only remembering his wife when he crossed the threshold to their apartment. This kind of cop – especially this kind of cop – was exactly the kind Vilya did not want to run into in this empty kitchen with its sink treacherously full of dishes.

Thus Vilya poured the bitter and unsweetened coffee into two cups and decided to change his plans for the immediate future. He had to get out of this apartment fast. Under any pretext. He'd get Dita's phone number, promise to call her as soon as he was back in Kiev, and get out this second …

Yet the moment he entered the bedroom he almost rejected that rational plan – the only one possible in his current position – so tempting was Aphrodita. She was already awake but still snuggled in the bed, waiting for his return. As if by chance – but not by chance at all, naturally – the blanket covered her in such a way as to remind Vilya instantly of the caressing press of her breasts as she had lain in his arms the night before, of the tender touch of her hips against his legs, and of the insistent movements of her lips and tongue.

"Ah, coffee…" Aphrodita stretched contentedly. Then she turned on her side and, after a brief moment, emerged from the bedclothes. She sat up on the bed, wrapped in a blanket to give the impression of covering up her slightly plump body – while at the same time covering up hardly any of it. Finally, she took the cup from Vilya, who all this time had stood before her, unsure where to put either his hand or the coffee cups.

Downing the slightly cooled coffee in one gulp, Vilya at last found the strength to turn down everything Dita was so eloquently, though silently, offering him.

Avoiding the disappointed look on her face, he told her he had to rush, that since he hadn't made his flight the night before he needed to get the morning one, and he was already running late for that as well. That if Dita would give him her phone number he would call her at the first opportunity, and as soon as he was back in Kiev they would see each other. That Kiev for him now was she, Dita, and he would definitely sing for her when they next met. Both "A-ap" and "City Flowers" – and anything else she would like. Vilya was compelled to speak quickly and briefly, or Dita, if she was the slightest bit resourceful, would silence him with one long kiss and undo his firm resolution.

She wrote her number on a piece of paper torn from a notepad close at hand. Shrugging on the dress she had worn the night before, she walked him to the door. She gave him a light peck goodbye, closed the door behind him, and for a long time watched him wait for the elevator through the eyehole: incredible, Boyarsky is standing on our humble landing, waiting for our elevator. Literally the same way we wait for it every morning. The thought of everything that had transpired before this was not something Aphrodita was ready to face at the moment.

The elevator door opened in front of Vilya and he waved goodbye to Aphrodita, as though he had known all along that she was watching him through the eyehole.

Exiting the elevator on the first floor, Vilya bumped into a tall and large blond man with curly, though thinning hair, who seemed vaguely familiar. But Vilya couldn't recall where and when he had seen him. Jonas Butenas, senior detective for the Department Against Misappropriation of Socialist Property, was just returning from a work trip to Vilnius two days earlier than expected. And he recognized Vilya. Not at first, but he remembered him because Vilya's photograph was in an open police file in his department, like those of all the Kiev speculators who had contact with foreigners. Captain Butenas wasn't surprised by their meeting, exactly, but it nonetheless gave him something to think about.

Summers in the Country, USSR 1965–1974

Avril Pyman

Born of a Methodist mother and Congregationalist father, I was christened Avril in the Church of England, in the Parish of Aislaby near Whitby, in the village of Dunsley where there was a convenient "Mission Room" which doubled as a school. My parents, *post factum*, decided I should be called Deryn, but it was the nickname Dicky that stuck. In 1963, the year I married the Russian artist Kirill Sokolov, I was accepted into the Eastern Orthodox Church as Maria. In the country, in Russia, you just had to have a Christian name and a patronymic, so I became Maria Fedorovna after the popular Queen Mother of the last Tzar. My father, needless to say, was no more Theodor than hers had been, but Frederick. "Fridrikovna," however, sounded more German than English (or - as in my illustrious predecessor's case – Danish) and, anyway, my father was known to friends and family by his second name, Cresswell (or Cressy) – which, as my mother-in-law wisely pointed out, sounded too like Croesus for anyone marrying into a Communist country. So "Maria Fedorovna" I became to everyone in Russia who did not already know me as Dicky, though remaining Avril plus maiden-name on my books and Avril plus Sokolov on my passport: a messy arrangement which led Russian readers to take me for a man – an analogy with Averell Harriman – and caused confusion with my credit card because of the masculine ending that I had registered as the surname for my new English passport after my wedding. It had seemed to me then that Sokolova was more suited to a ballerina than an academic, though I needn't have worried as – when it came to it – my students at Durham University were perfectly happy with Doc. Sock! The poor little Welsh "bird" (my mother was Gwenneth and there was an Aunt Myvfanwe, widowed and dug out of the rubble in the London blitz) had, by then, fallen by the wayside. Enough background …

So there I was, the author of these reminiscences, turning thirty-five in 1965, two years married and pregnant, looking for a "dacha"[1] where my husband and I could work on commission over the summer months, take a rest from our communal flat in Moscow and fill our lungs with fresh, country air. We had had a very pleasant arrangement in the outskirts of Zvenigorod during the first year of our marriage, but the authorities had refused to prolong the permit to reside anywhere other than at my registered address in Moscow – possibly because Zvenigorod was also the site of Brezhnev's private dacha and it was common gossip there that he had been holding meetings, plotting to overthrow Khrushchev and effect a rapprochement with China ... All I was told, by a disembodied, somewhat aggrieved voice on the telephone, was "We can't make out what you're doing there." ...

When we were forbidden Zvenigorod and after losing a cash deposit on other rooms in the semi-rural western suburbs of Moscow, also considered unsuitable by the Department of Visas and Registrations who decided such things, we spent some time and energy persuading them to give us an indication as to where we *could* go. Eventually, we were given the green light to see what we could find South East of the capital and within a thirty-kilometer radius, found maps and looked for water. On the way out to the airport at Domodedovo the road crosses a river, the Pakhra, on the forested banks of which Lenin once had <u>his</u> dacha.

From the bridge, our eyes were drawn the other way down river to a picturesque village called Kolychevo on the bank of the meandering water. It was, as the name suggested, the historical patrimony of the good sixteenth century Metropolitan Philip, murdered by Maliuta Skuratov for his brave opposition to the authoritarianism of his childhood friend Ivan the Terrible. We asked the bus to stop and

---

1   Air quality and heat are oppressive in Moscow during the summer and everyone who can gets away – or at least evacuates their children. There were "official" dachas for members of government, co-operative "villages" with dachas for writers, artists, scientists, professors, party officials, for so-called Old Communists and high-ranking retired military. Many people had relatives (often grandparents) in the country; or ordinary, undistinguished mortals like us could take advantage of an unofficial system of subletting: in the country it was quite common for peasants to let out the more comfortable winter part of their houses and retreat to the "*seni*" (the less hermetically sealable passageways, lofts and undercrofts of the "*izba*").

let us out, and set off on foot to see what we could find, knocking on doors.

"Nobody lets rooms here," we were told by a helpful housewife. "But you could try over there …" and she pointed down-river and away from the road to an abrupt bend and a line of forest with tiny wooden houses edging the wooded slope of the yonder bank.

"Oh," I said. "Let's go." "Don't be so stupid," snapped Kirill, thoroughly out of temper. "There's no road and you're going to have a baby." To one who had survived 1940-46 in an isolated Yorkshire hamlet and whose elder sister had had <u>three</u> babies there during war and petrol rationing, this was no argument at all. So we set off across the river and along a dirt track wide enough for farm vehicles to the distant village. An hour or so later we were knocking on the door of the first house we came to.

It was opened by one of the sweetest women I have ever met: Maria Ivanovna, the village post-woman, with soft, gray hair caught back from her face, slender as a young girl, lively, blue-grey eyes: "How can I help you? … Oh, rooms … oh, I'm so sorry, I've family coming for the summer. Maybe opposite. Maria Georgievna."

Maria Georgievna appeared at once, sturdy and hospitable, on her porch. There aren't many new arrivals in a village with no proper road to it. She was sorry, but she could not help either. Maybe Maria Nikiforovna up the hill…?

So off we set to seek out Maria Nikiforovna, who turned out to be very short, stout and lame, hobbling on two sticks. She had three grown-up sons, but one was working at the airport, the middle one had left the village altogether and the younger was in prison, so she could easily clear the main part of the house for us: "Come in, come in and see if it suits you."

We came in and it suited us. Kirill was deeply amused when our new "landlady" shooed him away and led me out conspiratorially to the very top of the hill at the back of the house, where her state-of-the-art outside earth closet was fitted with startlingly brilliant electric light you could turn on from the main house – all set up by the son from the airport. I was solemnly invited to try it out and, as I emerged, Maria Nikiforovna herself rose beaming from a clump of leggy cabbages and exclaimed triumphantly: "you – there, Maria Fedorovna, and I down here!"

A few weeks later we took a taxi along the track across the fields, loaded with provisions and everything we needed for the summer. There was no shop, but a van called with bread and groceries once a week and Maria Nikiforovna kept hens so there was a plentiful supply of fresh eggs. One could buy berries and vegetables direct from the villagers and Maria Georgievna had two cows and kept us plentifully supplied with beautiful fresh milk. "Not even TESTED!" exclaimed a lady from the British embassy. Then, softening slightly, "Well, I suppose as long as you know the cow…" We did, only there were two of them, one white, one brown: "Mil'ka" and "Zor'ka." Maria Georgievna paid the cowherd and gave him a good, hot meal once every so often at her home to graze them along the riverbank and through the neighboring glades and forest with the herd from the *Sovkhoz*.[2] The

2 Kupreyanikha was attached to a *Sovkhoz* or candidate to become a *Sovkhoz* or *State Farm* as opposed to a *Kholkoz* or *Collective Farm*, the economic units which had replaced the assortment of landowner estates, peasant communes and successful yeomen farmers (later branded *Kulaks* or *Fists*). The peasants, a word still in everyday use in Soviet times without archaic pejorative flavor to designate those who actually worked the land, owned their own homes with small front gardens for flowers and back gardens for vegetables and fruit. Not all bothered with the flowers. Some kept bees, others a cow or two, goats, even in some cases, a small horse. The State or Collective Farm owned all agricultural machinery, herds of cattle, flocks of domestic fowls, expanses of arable land and grazing, and had administrative control of housing and community services such as water supply, electricity etc. The police were far away, as was medical help. I never saw a policeman in the villages. There was a "Feldsher" (with qualifications between those of doctor and district nurse) in the neighboring village of Lukino (the Sanatorium was not for locals). In case of fire, one beat the "nabat" (an iron rail) to rally the villagers and form a chain of buckets. Though some things changed little, the law changed constantly. In the days of "War Communism," immediately after the First World War during the Civil War, "expropriators" from cities and industrial centers were sent in by the Soviets to commandeer produce, sometimes even seed grain, a policy which antagonized the peasants to the point of armed resistance. The New Economic Policy provided opportunities to grow comparatively rich, but weaker families went to the wall and began to form a "proletariat" of landless laborers and insecure smallholders. In the '30s, the "collectivization of agriculture" began in earnest with the introduction of State and Collective Farms, the confiscation of livestock and "the elimination of the Kulaks as a class." Consequent famine, then war, necessitated the re-introduction of a profit motive. It was still frowned on to employ hired labor, but a family could market their own produce, and regulations as to whether one might, with impunity, own one or two cows, were liable to change from one year to the next. Survival was a matter of second-guessing the authorities, keeping in step with the ever-changing

bull went with them and one kept out of their way as they mooed their way over the grassy street towards home, but Mil'ka and Zor'ka turned readily away from the rest to be fed and milked in their own stalls. The cowherd spent the entire day on horseback, his portable radio slung over his shoulder for company. There were moose in the forest, but the wolves, now the war had long ceased providing them with carrion, had betaken themselves further from the great cities. Maria Ivanovna's son, however, remembered with a shudder being followed by a lean gray shadow all the way home from the nearest bus-stop from school; telling himself, all along the river-bank, NOT TO RUN! The wolf never quite made up its mind to attack. Within twenty-five miles from Moscow, a degree of self-sufficiency was essential – even for a schoolboy.

We were very happy with Maria Nikiforovna. She told wonderful stories – not as a trained actor reads an audiobook but in a bardic singsong, with sudden elliptic descents into the vernacular. All her generation had been schooled by the nuns at the nearest village. "Lukino was always a monastic village, Kupreyanikha a sorcerers'. Never had our own Church." The nuns had taught them to read, write, and sing. Maria Ivanovna later taught Irina, our daughter, her notes, and to my surprise I came upon them singing: "Do, re, me, fa, so … !" – and not the *Sound of Music* version … Maria Nikiforovna told us how the convent, which was now a sanatorium, was disbanded in the early '30s. At the time, the local Party officials simply came and ordered the nuns out "and then those hooligans, the Komsomoltsy, were allowed to bring in rifles and make them run across the ploughed field. They didn't hurt them, but it was so funny to see them running in their long

---

rules and keeping one's head down. Small State farms such as the Kupreyanikha *Sovkhoz* had become something of a matriarchy. Few men had returned from the war and the "fatherless generation," who would naturally have succeeded them, tended to gravitate to more populous centers with better-paid jobs and more freedom of movement. It made sense to leave grandmother (who had kept things going during the war with minimum male help) resident in the family home so that there was still a place to belong, to enjoy a free holiday and to replenish a feeling for their own roots. None of our three Marias' children worked for the *Sovkhoz*.

skirts!" One nun ran to Kupreyanikha and married there, breaking her vows, for which she was struck blind: "Blind Nastya." But now she was a highly respected widow who knew all the prayers for the various necessities (*"treby"*) of country life. The nearest priest served a number of villages and was seldom available, so everyone would turn to Nastya in bereavement, sickness or want for specific prayers for which they had forgotten the words. She knew all the intercessions and blessings by heart, which was a good thing for the villagers who now had to bury their dead in an unhallowed stand of trees on the way to Lukino. The women would get together and sing for the repose of their souls on the various days set aside for remembering the dead. Maria Ivanovna was, rather surprisingly, particularly important here, because she was "the only one who knew the bass". It was important not only for spiritual reasons, but also to allay superstitious terrors. Neglected, the dead might grow hungry in their graves and waylay belated homecomers on the track from the main road …

"As for those new landowners, the Communists," Maria Nikiforovna concluded her history of the two villages, "they didn't always know what they were about. Elijah's Day, you know, was always a holiday, and they went and made the men harvest the corn. Well … there was a thunderstorm that night and all the stooks were carried away." "Maria Nikiforovna," I said, deeply impressed by her sepulchral tone and total disrespect for the powers that be, "Who carried the stooks away?" She took my measure with quick little eyes and replied, rather grumpily, "Who carried off the stooks? Why, the wind, of course. Who did *you* think? Elijah the Prophet?"

We loved Nikoforovna and she was well-disposed to us because Kirill had taken to the younger son, now released from forced labor with multiple sclerosis, and had done his best to get advice from the Medical Academy in Moscow, via his mother's contacts. She taught English at the Academy and did indeed know a specialist on that wretched, progressive illness. There was no cure, he confirmed the prison doctor's diagnosis, but one strange symptom he had noticed in the pursuit of one. The disease always seemed to afflict particularly likeable, sweet-natured people. His mother was delighted to learn this. Also, I trusted her, loved listening to her, and was always good for a laugh... unlike a previous lodger from the town who, she said, had done nothing but wash her linen every day and then "kept watch" as it dried on the line in case her landlady helped herself to the odd pair of voluminous, pink knickers. "*Stiraet i sterezhet! Tol'ko i delaet ... sterezhet i opiat' stiraet!*" ("Washing and watching! That's all she ever did ... watching and washing!")

I did as little washing as possible in those days. There was no running water and we had to bring it from a pump on the street and heat it in kettles on a paraffin stove, which also served for cooking. At the bend in the river at the bottom of the street was a wooden jetty from which one could either dive into the Pakhra for a refreshing swim or rinse one's laundry in the clear flowing stream. It struck both Kirill and me that life "on the hill" would be very arduous next summer. There would be nappies and baby clothes, so we decided we must move nearer the river and Maria Nikiforovna agreed. She had a word with our original two Marias, and it was Maria Georgievna who offered to accommodate us; Maria Ivanovna, with typical modesty, thinking her lovely little house not good enough for Kirill with his beautiful blue eyes, his paints, his easel, and his foreign wife. Maria Georgievna, however, decided I would fit in because I was not afraid of her cows, as ladies from the town tended to be. Also, her *izba* was larger than most, her son Vadik spent much time away and her hugely good-natured lorry-driver husband, Uncle Sanya, one of the few men of the village to have returned from the war, had no objection. Also, she loved babies. Once we were installed the following summer, Maria Nikiforovna would come down the hill almost every day for a chat with her friends, and to observe the progress of little Irochka. Maria Georgievna was a good neighbour. Maria Ivanovna was clearly unwell, not an ounce of spare flesh on her, and our new landlady invited her every day to drink a mug of milk warm from the cow. This was a proper invitation, not just an act of charity. Maria Georgievna would join her at table on the "terrace" and Maria Nikiforovna hobble down the hill to sit with them. Kirill sketched them, "The Three Marias," a courteous little gathering with compositional overtones of Rublev's Trinity.[3]

At the end of that first summer, though, I left Maria Nikiforovna's for Moscow standing up in the back of a very bouncy lorry, watched with fascinated horror over every bounce by Kirill and his great friend Sasha Ershov, but managed to hang on to the baby and produce her on time back in England some three months later on December 9. My mother had died the previous year. In a dream, she had been the first to tell me that I was expecting, which she discovered by gently touching my temples with a caressing movement I had particularly loved as a child. My father, who had Parkinsonism and probably the beginning of Alzheimer's (he was certainly very forgetful and kept himself in the know by writing everything down and constantly referring back to his diary), was the first to turn up at the nursing home while I was still puffing and panting from the birth. "They've just shown me your little girl! She looked at me as though she understood *everything!*" So beautiful … He came to see us the following summer in Moscow accompanied by my cousin Eve, otherwise known as Sunshine (or Soapsud) Sue. There was a hold-up in the foyer of the hotel Ukraine because of some misunderstanding with bookings and considerable excitement among the milling new arrivals when a journalist mistook Daddy for the Duke of Wellington, due to clock in at the same time. It was Irochka's lusty wails rather than Cressy's silver hair, imposing height and general air of antiquated authority, however, which got him and cousin Eve priority in the bookings scramble and saw them (and us) to a decent suite – after much whispering and maternal cluckings between the ladies on reception. Eve was too relieved to escape the logjam in the foyer to object to doubling up, although pleased to discover she was not actually expected to share a bed with her uncle!

---

3 Two of Kirill's formalized oil paintings of the Trinity and one original watercolor of the three Marias and Uncle Sanya at table are now installed behind the high table of St Chad's beautiful dining room at Durham University. The sketches were gifted to the Vladimir Propp folklore section of Saint Petersburg University after an exhibition arranged at the Nabokov Museum *ensuant* on an illustrated talk at a conference in Durham on "Death in Russian Culture." The rough charcoal sketches reproduced here remain in the K. K. Sokolov Archive.

The weather was dry so we were able to get a taxi to Kupreyanikha to show Daddy our beautiful summer retreat and he pleased all who met him by being just what they expected of an Englishman: unable to communicate, of course, but tall, spare, humorous, and as sportif as his years would allow. He died later that year and our little family - orphaned in a foreign land – was gifted with generous supplies of portable country fare from the gardens of our village friends. I was overcome, sniffling all the way back to Moscow, and Kirill too was touched and surprised to find us the object of such generous sympathy.

It was for our third summer that we finally settled in with our first friend, Maria Ivanovna. I was offering a modest wage to free myself up for work by keeping an eye on my now toddling daughter; Maria Ivanovna's health could no longer support the post-round in all weathers; and we had been vetted by Liza, Zina, and Tolya, her robust, vivid grown-up children, whom she had raised alone (her husband died on active service), as she herself put it, "on carrots and fresh air." All three were married: Zina, blonde, big, and curly-haired, to Geisha, an ambulance driver at the Sanatorium at Lukino. The job provided them with a flat and all mod cons. Liza, big, dark, and quieter than her rumbustious sister, lived in the industrial spread to the East of Moscow with her husband, Ivan, a police-dog trainer. Tolya, fair-haired like Zina, tall and remarkably good-looking, had a flat in Greater Moscow with his wife Rita, an engineer, and their silvery-blonde little son, Serezha. It was Maria Ivanovna's fondest boast that Tolya, a trained technician, worked "in a white overall," and it was to his hospitable flat that Kirill and I were invited to meet all three families. It was a wonderfully entertaining evening. A table laden with festive food and drink encouraged animated conversation, stories from real life which Kirill readily capped with hospital stories: "always go down well," he would say, "and everybody has one or two of their own!" As the food dwindled, they sat back and began to sing. Tolya had a pleasant baritone and a great repertory, Zina a powerful Slavic soprano. The others joined in ... harmonizing. We just listened, enchanted. "Grief is no ocean. All will ease, pass away ..." Old songs, new songs, heartfelt, funny ... On the way home, Kirill said wonderingly: "What a marvelous evening. That lot have twice the talent of the Intelligentsia," which, from him was saying something … his family and friends all seemed to be professional artists, musicians, architects, writers … Still, my husband was a man of enthusiasms and he had made a discovery, or, perhaps, a rediscovery. Townspeople everywhere in the world have lost contact with traditional culture – and it is a loss indeed. Kirill's occasional sketches were turning into a pictorial account of the life of a Moscow-district *Sovkhoz* – very different from the politico-promotional "socialist-realist" dream …[4]

Meanwhile, we had the good fortune to be adopted not only into the house of Maria Ivanovna but, to some extent, at least for her lifetime, into her family. Admittedly, she only bore with life in Moscow with us for one winter: "I don't know why it is, Maria Fedorovna, I love your Irochka and you and Kirill Konstantinovich are so good to me, sometimes better than my own family, and everything's so clean and easy … But I can't bear it, I miss my home. I've just got to go back. I'll see if I can't find someone else to help you next winter …" I regret to say that Irochka hid under the table from her unobjectionable successor, from which safe sanctuary she turned round and said in robust Kupreyanikha Russian: "Fuck your mother, I don't WANT to go for a walk." "That wasn't a very nice thing to say," I remonstrated (she and I spoke English). "But Auntie Zina says it," she replied – adding shrewdly: "I suppose it's all right for her because she's grown-up, is it?" Aunty Zina we had witnessed in particularly fine form that summer. As Kirill, Ira, and I strolled by the river, there was a sudden explosion of shrieks and shouts from up the hill, where a convivial gathering was taking place; a young man tore past us towards the wooden jetty, his legs running away with him on the steep slope, Geisha and Tolya in hot pursuit. "Your watch!" shrieked Zina as Geisha pounded past. He took it off without breaking his strike and flung it at her. The youth rose to the surface and was striking out high in the water in a magnificent crawl towards

---

4   The series has turned out to be a swan song. Kupreyanikha has been all but swallowed by greater Moscow, the wooden houses almost all superseded by walled "dachas"; bolted gates bear the legend "Beware of the Dog"; the road has been hard-surfaced. Only a few village families remain, most looking for a way out. What has happened to the *Sovkhoz* I do not know.

the far bank, but, almost immediately, began to choke and sink. Within seconds Geisha and Tolya were hauling him back onto the bank and laying him out on the grass for the tender ministrations of Zina, who proceeded to pump the water out of him, showering him with a string of obscenities which Ira, secure in her father's arms, was absorbing with all the riveted interest of a robin inspecting a whole trayful of tasty birdseed. We never disentangled the full story behind the incident. It looked more like a silly bet gone wrong than a suicide attempt, but the rescue was, nevertheless, impressive. Geisha was last seen sheepishly strapping on his wristwatch and heading back up hill with Tolya to see if Maria Ivanovna had any spare dry clothes for large men ...

Drink was usually at the bottom of such affrays, which featured high comedy rather than tragedy – except in the case of Nikiforovna's younger son, who had, some years ago, taken a pot shot at his successful rival on his wedding day, but blinded in one eye, by mistake, the bride he had wanted for himself, and been sentenced to forced labor ... the entire village insisting loyally that he was normally the gentlest and most obliging character on the hill ...

Another occasion featuring Zina was a fight in the woods with the men of a neighboring village – something in the nature of a ritual clash between rival football fans. It had started as a friendly picnic, which was why we were there. Zina decided to break up a sudden tussle among the men, slipping off her sandals and moving into the thick of the fray, swearing like a trooper and slapping painfully left-right with the soles. Her brother kept her back, walking hard up behind her, serviceable fists seconding the flapping sandals from around her body ... I headed for home before Ira could pick up any more choice expressions; Kirill helped calm the situation with a diversion involving the heave-ho of some kind of hand-cart into the river ... and they all went home again ...

Dostoyevsky tells a wonderful tale of how once, as a little boy on holiday, he had run from a wolf into the safe embrace of a friendly peasant: the huge reassurance of the man's strength and good will ... the relief that he knew what to do and understood the danger. I experienced two similar moments:

The first involved a somewhat quixotic attempt on our part to join in some winter celebration in Kupreyanikha. For some reason, Kirill made the journey either before or after Ira and me. She, I think, must have been about three, and I decided to pull her and the usual bundle of provisions on her little sleigh (the Moscow winter substitute for a pushchair and much more serviceable on the snow-covered dirt-track from Lukino to Kupreyanikha). There was a well-tended asphalt road from the bus stop on the *chaussée* to the sanatorium but, after Lukino, an unfenced track coasted gently down through the unfenced fields. I had reckoned without the snow. Everything looked different and, at an unrecognized fork in the track, I chose the clearly more used, downhill branch, only to arrive some twenty minutes later at a steaming manure heap – and a dead end. By the time we were back at the fork we had lost more than an hour, the short, winter day was closing in, and it was beginning to snow. I hurried past the grave-wood, conscious of my delicious child perched among fragrant salamis and hunks of cheese, pluckily singing along behind me – unfortunately, I cannot keep a tune, but still sang lustily to cheer us along: "*Glor-oria, glor-oria, glor-or-or-or-oria, in excelsis Deo!*" and other such seasonal processionals. Still, I could not quite drown out the memory of Tolya's shadowy, gray wolf. My shortsighted eyes were half-blinded with snow and the dark was falling fast. Moreover, the snow seemed to be getting deeper and softer at every step and it was really very cold. I had begun to worry we might have missed the track again when, suddenly, there was music, lights, a chorus of friendly voices from behind. Uncle Sanya, crimson-cheeked from the frost, driving a sleigh with a shaggy little horse from the *Sovkhoz*; anxious voices; helping hands. "Maria Fedorovna, what are you doing out here in the dark?" "Give us that child!" "That's right, Irochka. Hoopla!" "Tie that little sleigh to ours. There we go, you hop in too." We're almost home!" And we were …

The next occasion was also about weather. A summer story. There was a sandy stretch of shore with shallow water up-river from the Kupreyanikha bend. It was very hot, and I had taken Irochka and Serezha, dressed in nothing but sun-pants, for a paddle. I wore a bathing dress under a sundress and we had one towel between us. There were several other people lounging in the sand. It really was too hot to work! A black cloud advanced on us against the wind and the others began to drift away – but I took no notice, lazily absorbed in the children's game. They were industriously baking a feast of sand-pies, addressing one another as "husband" and "wife" like an elderly couple from another age of the world. Then came a loud clap of thunder, right over our heads. I gathered up our scant belongings and the hail hit us as we reached the path: - huge pebbles of ice. The children were squealing pathetically and I laid them down, spread the inadequate towel over as much as it would cover and lay on top of them. It seemed to be easing off, so we got up and hurried for home, me carrying Serezha who was, understandably, crying for his mum; Ira, as usual, staunchly co-operative but silent, all three of us by now thoroughly scared. Just as the hail intensified again a large, familiar figure came swinging towards us from the village, carrying extra blankets – Zina's husband, Geisha. He wrapped the children like sausage rolls, threw a third blanket over my bare shoulders and, tucking a child beneath each arm, headed for home, chortling soothingly. We fought our way back to the house, where the shivering youngsters endured a vigorous rubdown with neat vodka – and Geisha and I were awarded a generous slug apiece of the same panacea.

So, after the happy winter (for us) in Moscow with Maria Ivanovna, who made us more friends than we ever deserved in our new Union of Journalists Co-operative ground-floor flat, we continued to spend the summers in her house. She taught Irochka to be generous and open-handed with her sweets and toys, to recite a whole litany of lively Russian *chastushki* (improvised, calypso-type jingles) and, when greeted with one of those meaningless grown-up "how are you's," not to lower her eyes and mumble, but to look up with a smile and reply smartly with the equivalent of "I'm *fine*, thank you. And how are you?" A model of courtesy herself, she also taught us to be polite to people tapping on the kitchen window (which was beside the locked entrance) asking for plastic bags (not available over the counter at that time), or even small loans to buy some (usually edible) rarity, unexpectedly on display in the shops, or to be let in to visit their friends on the ninth floor up! She had the great politeness to remind me to *offer* her butter at the breakfast table: "No, Maria Fedorovna, I would *never* help myself!"

Unforgettably, she *did* help herself to a book of folk tales by a supposedly difficult surrealist émigré writer, a great connoisseur of the spoken Russian idiom, Aleksey Remizov. He was considered a difficult author, for specialists only, but had his admirers in the Soviet Union and some followers among Soviet writers (Boris Pilnyak, Andrey Platonov, and others). I had already lost one or two rare Parisian and pre-Revolutionary Russian editions of his works to absent-minded Moscow bibliophiles and, looking worriedly up and down our bookshelves, asked Maria Ivanovna, quite unsuspectingly, whether she had seen this particular book. "Oh, Maria Fedorovna," she replied uncomfortably, "I took it – it's at Kupreyanikha – to read to the women on the stove.[5] What do you learned people want with folk tales? – We love them and you can't get ones like that nowadays. Real good ones!"

The *Tales* were, eventually, returned – though with a reluctance that would have delighted their "difficult" author, who I had known when studying in Paris and, alas, never got to tell about it. He had died in 1957, complaining bitterly to the last that reviewers seemed to think he chose to write in Russian-as-it-is-spoken-in-and-around Moscow "just in order to make my books harder to understand" …

I think it must have been the winter of 1970 or 1971 that Maria Ivanovna died. It was not our season for country living, but Kirill and I, of course, went to the funeral. It had been to save up for this eventuality that Maria Ivanovna had agreed to stay the winter with us and to care for Ira in the summer months: to avert expense for her children and avoid any possible bad feeling over who should pay for what after she died …

They did her proud. By the time we arrived the winter part of the house, which had been given over to our use in the summer, had been completely cleared of furniture except for a bed with the open coffin on it placed diagonally in a corner by

---

5   The Russian stove is a tiled quadrilateral reaching from floor to ceiling which, in winter, acts as oven and central heating for the *izba*. It has a heated space, used as a bed for the sick or play-space for the children, above the log-fuelled oven part. It was Ira's delight to be helped "onto the stove" to dry when we washed her hair. Maria Ivanovna would creep up with her and read her a story, snuggled down on "Liuska," a goatskin from a beloved defunct pet of Tolya, Liza and Zina. I remember one of those "who loves who best in the world?" conversations and Irochka's beaming, little face looking down at us: "I love *myself*. Look at me, all warm and curly."

the window. All the village was there and, of course, her children. Zina stood by their mother's bedside and talked to her loud and clear: not an intimate murmuring but an improvised performance for all the room to hear:

"Look, mother, look, how many people have come to see you off. There's Tolya and Liza with Ivan and here's Kirill Konstantinovich with Maria Fedorovna come all the way from Moscow …"

So it went on, a long, loving commentary, until there was a sudden stir and her menfolk came forward to carry out the coffin. We all followed and it was laid down, briefly, before each of the two houses in which she had lived, before being put into the hearse (a large designed-for-purpose van with RITUAL written on the side) and taken to the church in Kolychevo, followed by a bus with the mourners. Kirill and I were honored to be transported together with the family and the body. Zina went on talking to her all the way:

> You wanted to make your confession, but we said: "Whatever have you got to confess, Mother? You've got no sins." But she said: "Oh yes I have. When Tolya was born I never took a prayer[6] for him and now he's losing his way … it's my fault." So I told her: "There's no-one as good as you, Mother. Do you remember how you taught us you must always give to the first three beggars you meet on your way to church? If you have no money, give bread; no bread – give a potato or whatever there is to eat. But, if you've really got nothing – don't hurry past but look them in the eye and just say: 'Sorry, love, but I've nothing myself.'" …

And so she went on till the van came to a halt and the men rallied round again to bear the coffin into the church where it was laid on a plinth and Liza and Zina together began the lament.

This was traditional ritual and painful to listen to, the sisters working each other up into hysteria with howls and yelps and cries of "Mother, Mother, why have you left us? Why? Why?"

---

6   Although Orthodox I am not sure whether this refers to some special prayer the priest speaks over a new mother and child or the ceremony of "Churching" the woman after the birth or even of baptizing the baby, though my instinct is that one way or another she would have managed this last – even in the isolation of the country in wartime.

Then, as if from nowhere, the choir struck up, the same women who had regularly visited the graves with Maria Ivanovna intoning "the bass." "Holy God, Holy and Strong, Holy and Immortal, have mercy upon us..."[7] The voices seemed to absorb and raise up the raw desolation of the lament, transporting us all beyond time, space, and death itself, and, to the sound of the singing, the coffin was carried, followed by the mourners in solemn procession, to the waiting vehicles. We went with the family to the woodland graveyard, where the coffin was put down for the last time on wooden struts. Ivan looked with quiet eyes at the small, delicate face: "Nu[8] Maria Ivanovna," and covered it for the last time. The lid was gently placed over it and he hammered in the first nail. The coffin was lowered into the ready-dug grave, earth quietly scattered.

We had to leave immediately after the cemetery to get back to Moscow but, most surely, Maria Ivanovna's fellow-villagers returned to her home and, as she would have wished, to a slap-up wake.

---

7   "The Trisagion" is an ancient Orthodox hymn sung at funerals as the body is carried round the Church and out for the Committal. It is also sung at the heart of the Liturgy and at the beginning of the *panikhida* (memorial service) and so is equally at home in a deeply personal and in a corporate context.

8   "Nu" is an everyday expression meaning anything from "Now" to "Time's up" to "Well, now." In context, the homely monosyllable had a strangely solemn, yet affectionate, finality.

The Three Marias by Kirill Sokolov

Maria Ivanana and Maria Georgievna by Kirill Sokolov

"Blind" Nastia by Kirill Sokolov

Maria Nikiforovna by Kirill Sokolov

Nature Notes
A Selection of Sketches from *Travels* and *A Hunter's Stories*

Ivan Sokolov-Mikitov

Translated from the Russian
by Kevin Windle

Aerial Combat

As I looked out over a bay covered in birds, I caught sight of a peregrine falcon. The powerful short-winged bird was flying low over the surface of the water. In skimming flight it rushed over a mass of birds. Taken unaware, the ducks feeding on the surface quickly dived. Along the falcon's line of flight a broad path cleared all by itself on the water.

In the middle of the bay the peregrine swooped at a group of plump black coots. Startled by the sudden assault, the foolish birds attempted to take wing. The falcon began manoeuvring with extraordinary agility. Making steep turns, the fast, short-winged raptor tried to prise the coots from the water, circling and diving like a fighter-plane.

I raised my field-glasses to observe the aerial combat more closely. Now I could see all the movements of the birds. The clumsy coots, forced into the air, rose higher and higher. The falcon seemed to be making fun of them.

I followed the deadly game. Suddenly the peregrine changed direction, soared up like a rocket into the sky above the coots, and having gained height plummeted down on the panicking, scattering birds. A coot struck by a blow somersaulted in the air and began falling helplessly. After a sudden turn, the falcon stooped at another coot which had become separated from the flock. The aerial gladiator was performing loops and dives. As I watched I was reminded of airmen controlling their winged machines with the same level of skill.

The peregrine dealt very quickly with the flock. The downed birds fell on the shore and in the water. The raptor hardly needed to make any use of its quarry. It was killing for the sake of reveling in its agility and power.

The White-tailed Eagle

On a sandbar in the avian feeding-grounds stood the towering form of a white-tailed eagle, motionless for hours on end, like a stone idol, only occasionally turning its head, as if keeping order in the great kingdom of birds.

Around it countless flocks of birds seethed, stirred, and called. They apparently had no fear of the immobile idol. Paying no heed to the awe-inspiring eagle, they scurried right round its feet. Leaving the imprint of their beaks in the liquid ooze, long-legged sandpipers darted quickly about, and ducks of all kinds and colors preened and titivated their plumage. A white egret strutted self-importantly right under the eagle's bill. I gazed at length at this crowded world of birds, which seemed to me a magnificent theater.

"What is an enormous motionless eagle doing in this world?" I wondered. "What is its role in this grand performance?"

But at last the eagle began to stir, spread its huge wings and rise heavily into the air. It flew as far as the shore, where some gulls were sharing their booty on the tide-line, apparently a large dead fish cast up by the waves. The gulls were fastidious about carrion, and pecked reluctantly at the rotten fish.

Having driven off the gulls, the eagle started pecking eagerly at the meal stolen from them. I watched in astonishment as it made the most of the orts. My first impression had been so deceptive. This majestic and formidable bird was leading the wretched life of a beggar, reduced to the most shameful of roles and despised by other birds.

Pelicans

Returning to our cottage, I followed the bank of a creek brimming with spring floodwater. The remaining reeds concealed me from the birds feeding on the sandbars.

As I approached the water, I heard a loud commotion. At first I thought that somewhere an express train was passing at full steam. I made cautiously towards the source of the sound, through the reeds and over a dried-out saltpan. The closer

I approached, the clearer were the strange noises. They would grow louder, as if the train were very close, then suddenly die away, and in the silence I could hear the cries and cackles of birds.

Recalling my observations of long before, I thought to myself, "A big shoal of fish must have come close inshore, and the pelicans are hunting them."

At the mouth of the creek, where it entered the bay, I saw some pelicans. The huge white birds had ranged themselves in an arc, blocking the entrance to the shallow bay. At intervals, as if on command, they would start beating the water with their wings. From a distance the noise sounded like a train. They were driving a shoal of fish onto a sand-bank. The water in the shallows seemed to be boiling. A flock of black cormorants had grasped the opportunity and were circling over the water, which was teeming with fish, and descending onto it. The droving pelicans were advancing towards the sand-bank, allowing no breaks in their hunting chain. Hiding in the reeds, I saw the seething water and the greedy cormorants throwing back their heads as they tossed their live prey in the air.

Having herded the fish onto the sandbank, the pelicans began hastily packing their quarry into their pouches, which expanded, like elastic. When their pouches were full of live, struggling fish, the birds lumbered heavily into the air and gained height. One large white pelican flew low over me, weighed down by its catch. I fired a shot into the air, not wishing to kill it. Startled by the shot, it flapped its wings harder and dropped the catch from its pouch. A big struggling fish fell at my feet, as if the pelican wished to repay me for its freedom.

At the Roding Ground

Evening in the springtime forest is splendid. Overhead, the finest filigree of birch twigs, studded with buds about to open, is outlined sharply against the golden sky. On the bare treetops, as if vying with one another, the newly-arrived thrushes burst into song. Springing up from a patch of marshland and rising like an arrow into the sky, a snipe begins to drum.

Evening descends silently over the forest fringe.

Laying his shotgun across his lap, the hunter lights his pipe and harkens to

71

the numberless voices of the forest. The spring arrivals, the thrushes, sing out ever louder and clearer. The snipe rises higher and higher in the sky. The air is filled with the scent of decomposing leaves, of last year's grass, wild rosemary, and moss. Frogs awaken and trill tirelessly in puddles of translucent water. It is as if mysterious and ceaseless sounds were rising from the very earth itself. On a swaying branch nearby a hazel-grouse alights and gives its whistling cry.

The fiery orb of the sun sinks down beyond the river, lighting up the boles of the birches. High in the sky, small diaphanous clouds dissipate, as if heated. And the untiring thrushes sing with ever more power and feeling.

A brace of teal slice through the evening air overhead. Before you can raise your gun, the swift birds are gone, gliding over the latticework of the treetops.

A strange sound is heard from an alder carr beyond the glade: a blackcock, red-browed and clad in his black finery, has taken wing and flies over the trees. His call to arms resounds in the glade: "Chooff, chooff!"

Some evenings in spring are particularly enchanting. The sun-warmed dells seem to exude the warm breath of the earth itself, enveloping the hunter in living warmth, as from its opened bosom, after its long winter slumber.

On such warm, still evenings, the woodcock usually begin their roding early. The summits of the birches are still aflame when the hunter hears their familiar and thrilling call. Among the many other sounds of the forest, he can clearly distinguish the low croak and rapid chirrup of the oncoming bird.

Lit up by the rays of the setting sun, with unhurried flaps of its wings, the first woodcock glides over the woodland edge.

The very appearance of this forest bird has much charm about it. Its flight is singularly light, graceful, and silent. Its large dark eyes are beautiful, and its slender bill resembles the long blade of a rapier.

A woodcock brought down by an accurate shot is sometimes hard to find. Its forest plumage blends so well into the colors of the dead leaves. It takes the keen, trained eye of a seasoned marksman to find a winged bird quickly and unerringly, when it has come down in undergrowth beyond the trees. Inexperienced hunters waste much time trying to find their quarry, and let pass other woodcock which fly over with impunity during those annoying minutes.

The roding continues until it is completely dark. One needs to be able to choose one's spot faultlessly, sensing the birds' line of flight. Every experienced hunter has his favorite place, to which he hurries as soon as the season opens.

Woodcock-shooting at the roding site is not considered particularly difficult by most hunters, but that view is not always correct. On cold and windy days the birds fly fast, high and erratically. On such days not every hunter is able to hit a woodcock.

To the avid hunter who is bereft of any sense of poetry, to whom the measure of success is the number and total weight of his trophies, shooting at roding woodcock is not of great interest, of course. But the alert and observant hunter experiences a special sensation in spring. The spring roding gives him a poetic pleasure: the forest reveals to him its innermost secrets.

Swallows, Martins, and Swifts

As a child I loved watching the merry, fast-flying swallows. On a hot July day you could hide in tall ripening rye, or on a river bank in scented grass, amid an unmown flowering meadow, and gaze endlessly at the blue summer sky with fluffy white clouds sailing across it. High up, beneath the clouds, rapid white-breasted martins would wheel and bathe in the air, while sharp-winged swifts sped past with a ringing whistle.

Above your head, white and golden meadow flowers sway, butterflies float, light dragonflies hang motionless in the air with translucent wings aflutter, and grasshoppers trill. On green stalks crawl little red, yellow and black-spotted beetles – ladybirds, and ants dart busily along unseen pathways round the roots of the plants.

Every summer merry white-breasted martins would build their nests under the high eaves of the house where I spent my childhood. I would watch closely while they took mud from the fringes of a damp puddle and carried it in their beaks to fashion their tidy little homes from it. Later I would gaze in wonder as they hatched and fed their young. You could wake up in a hayloft under a thatched roof, where barn swallows had made their open, cup-shaped mud nests on the wooden beams. The long-tailed birds would dive through the doorway and keep flying right over your head. I could see close up how they clung to the edge of the nest and fed their young, who greeted their parents with cheery and lively chirrups.

I suppose everybody knows that there are urban swallows, or house martins, and rural swallows. Their lives are linked with human life. The urban whitebreasted birds – the house martins – make their cozy closed nests under the eaves of brick or wooden buildings, while barn swallows nest under the roofs of barns, byres, and sheds. They attach their open mud nests to wooden joists and ledges on wooden walls and under roofs. They fly nimbly through open gates and doorways, and the open windows of old abandoned buildings. Both swallows and martins feed exclusively on insects. They spend almost all their lives in the air, on the wing. With their wide gape they adroitly catch flying insects.

The barn swallow is particularly handsome. Its tail is adorned with two long streamers, and it sings beautifully. It will perch on a gable-top, flutter its long streamers and start twittering its simple but very pretty song. I recall how peasants, good-naturedly teasing their wives, used to translate that song into human language:

Menfolk off to work the fields –
The women to eat omelettes …
Menfolk off to work the fields –
The women to eat omelettes …

House martins live not only in towns, where there are plenty of brick buildings. They also live in villages alongside barn swallows. They live very sociably together, never squabbling or preventing others from building their nests. Sometimes a cheeky sparrow may enter a swallow's nest. Then the swallows will fuss round it, trying to expel the intruder. Sometimes they may desert a nest taken over by sparrows and start building another one beside it.

Before a change in the weather, or before a thunderstorm, swallows will fly low over the ground. You can be following a track across fields, and long-tailed swallows will fly fast and low over it, catching insects just above the ground. One often sees swallows flying low over the surface of a pond or a broad, lazy river. Their breasts will skim the water, leaving spreading circles of ripples. Thus they bathe and drink on the wing. I know no more appealing birds than our swallows. By their swift flight they enliven a dull and rainy sky, or a bright summer sky. Humans have long had warm feelings for swallows and given them affectionate names.

In addition to barn swallows and house martins, we also have sand martins. They make their nests in steep sandy banks, boring deep burrows in them. Sand martins usually fly very low over the water. They can be told from house martins and barn swallows by their gray-brown plumage.

Swallows and martins winter in far-off equatorial Africa and return every year to their homeland. At the end of summer, before their departure, they gather in small flocks and can be seen sitting on telephone and telegraph wires, and bare branches hanging low over water. They return home later than other migratory birds. As country folk used to say, "The swallow brings summer on its tail."

I remember how in my distant childhood I once saw martins fluttering in great agitation over the roof of our house, which stood amid deep forest. Now they would alight on the roof, now fly up. It was clear that something had happened. My friend Sashka the shepherd boy clambered up onto the roof and saw that one white-breasted bird had its claw caught in a chink in the woodwork. The other birds were anxiously trying to free it. Sashka detached it from the roof and climbed down. We could see that one leg was broken and hanging helplessly. I bound the leg it with a piece of cloth and put the bird a box lined with soft cotton wool. For some while it stayed with me, then flew off out of the window. I would often see it with its bandaged broken leg hanging when it flew to its nest. The most surprising thing was that that bird returned the next summer. I recognized it by its broken leg. It is hard to understand how so many migratory birds, including swallows, find their way to their old nests. Over forests, seas, high mountains, and vast steppes they fly many thousands of versts, and unfailingly find the place where they were born.

Besides the swallows and martins we all know, in summer we can see fast-flying swifts in the sky. These long-winged black birds, whistling as they fly overhead, also spend their whole lives on the wing, never alighting on the ground. If a swift is caught and placed on the bare ground, it cannot fly up. On its very short legs it is unable to walk on the ground.

Swifts usually frequent high belfries, stone buildings and tall trees. To take wing, the swift falls from its nest or a high ledge into the air, opening its wings in the air to launch into headlong flight. It is well known that swifts are the fastest of birds. They arrive even later than swallows, and at the end of summer disappear in the space of a day, as if on a word of command.

Crossbills

Of all the songbirds of the Russian forests, crossbills are perhaps the most interesting. In winter you may be skiing through the silent forest, admiring its fabulous beauty. Dark spruces rise above you, their boughs cloaked in snow. The slender boles of young birches are bent over under its weight, so that they resemble latticework lych-gates. The low winter sun lights up the treetops. There is hardly a sound to be heard in the dormant forest. Occasionally a busy woodpecker will tap and flit between the tree-trunks. A mass of light snow will fall from a broad spruce limb and shatter in diamond-like flakes; and the dark-green limb, freed from the weight, will sway above your head like a living thing. Your light skis whisper over the powdery snow and the winter forest seems even quieter than before.

Suddenly the silence is broken by some soft but merry bird calls. A small flock of crossbills flies over, adorning the top of a fir tree and its violet cones with bright beads of red. These red-breasted birds, which enliven the silence of the forest, are astonishingly beautiful. One stands in wonder, watching them tearing quickly and nimbly at the heavy cones to pick out the seeds. One after another the torn cones fall in the snow.

Crossbills are unusual among all the birds which winter in our forests in that they build their nests in winter and rear their young in the bitter cold of January and February. Their warm nests are difficult to see, as they are usually hidden deep in the dense needles of coniferous trees. The females lay their eggs and incubate them to hatching in winter. While they are laying and sitting, they do not leave their deep, snug nests. The male assiduously feeds the sitting female. Perched on the crown of the nest tree, he serenades his mate with a brief, merry little song.

I was once in the forest when some timber-cutters felled a tall spruce with many branches. A pair of crossbills fluttered anxiously over the fallen tree and the heads of the loggers. When I inspected it closely, I found a deep nest in the dense branches close to the trunk. Three small eggs lay on a soft, warm lining. I felt sorry for the hard-working little birds flying above our heads and their fallen tree. I also felt sorry for the green tree itself, which had given shelter to the crossbills. In winter they have no food but spruce and pine seeds, which they deftly tear out from the cones with the crossed mandibles of their rather parrot-like beaks.

I have never kept these handsome, jolly birds in captivity, but I have heard from people who have that they quickly grow accustomed to their human keepers. When kept in cages, they can be handled, and enjoy being stroked gently on the head, like parrots. Fed on fresh cones placed in their cage every day, they can be seen speedily dispatching them and picking out the small seeds. Tame crossbills may be fed on other kinds of seed, but in captivity the males soon lose their winsome bright coloration.

Observant people have long remarked that dead crossbills which have lived entirely on resinous conifer seeds do not decay for a long time. The dead body seems to be embalmed by the resin. There was a time when simple folk held crossbills to be sacred birds, a belief supported by their cruciform beaks. The merry crossbills which inhabit our coniferous forests are of two kinds: the red crossbill, which lives in spruce forest, and the parrot crossbill of the tall pine forest. Parrot crossbills can successfully pick out the seeds from pine cones.

If you happen to be in the depths of a spruce or pine forest in winter, you are almost certain to see jolly groups of handsome crossbills and hear their soft, pleasing calls. Of course, one has to walk quietly and pay attention to every sound. If you do, many wonderful secrets of the forest will be revealed to you, secrets of which the city-dweller, inexperienced and deafened by the din about him, is completely unaware.

Golden Orioles

Of all the songbirds, the musicians of the forests, the golden yellow oriole is the most secretive and the most beautiful.

Orioles live in pure birch groves, in old and shady parkland and avenues of tall oaks and lindens. In spring they appear late, when the trees are already decked in green and all the woodland songbirds have long since arrived.

Who has not heard the oriole's loud whistle in a birch grove? It sounds as if some unknown musicians were playing unseen musical instruments in the woodland.

The oriole's nest, artfully suspended in green boughs, is hard to find. One does not always manage to see the fabulous bird itself at close range, flying elusively from tree to tree. Only occasionally, when it flies across an open sunlit glade, does it flash its brilliant plumage.

Snow Buntings

In the far, far North, on the shores and islands of the uninhabited Arctic Ocean, I have had occasion to watch these charming little birds. There may still be deep snow on the ground, and sometimes freezing blizzards raging, but the snow buntings will have arrived, the first joyous harbingers of the Arctic spring. When the midnight sun is shining over the tundra without setting, and the snow is sparkling in it, the merry buntings twitter and flutter as they harvest their meager food on the first thawed patches.

At one time snow buntings nested in the least accessible of regions, in rock crevices in the bare, uninhabited tundra, but now they are found ever closer to human habitation, to the towns and settlements which have sprung up in the Far North of our country. Sometimes on emerging from the doorway of a polar research station, you hear its cheery and joyful call close at hand above the howling blizzard.

"Snow buntings! The snow buntings have arrived!"

Snow buntings live in close harmony with humans. They often build their nests under the eaves of houses. On the remote Taimyr Peninsula, at the mouth of the Lower Taimyr River, we observed many of them in spring at a polar station. These birds found refuge from the cold in a deep snow tunnel cut out beside the larder.

Snow buntings are small and very lively birds. Their short, jolly, cheerful song makes a friendly welcome. In winter in the Far North, when the sun hides from sight and the dark polar night sets in, the snow buntings fly south, but in early spring they invariably return to their cold homeland, where in spring and summer the midnight sun shines without setting. Beside our polar station we found a nest woven into the chassis of an old tracked vehicle. I observed the cheery little birds at close range while they fed their nestlings, which lived in a small, warm nest lined with soft down. Their busy parents caught food for their young in the tundra, bringing insects, including the tiresome mosquitoes that hung in dark clouds above our heads.

I do not know if snow buntings can be kept in captivity, but I believe that they will quickly grow accustomed to humans and be trustful of them. As I recall my travels long ago in the countries of the Arctic, I always remember merry snow buntings bringing life to the wonderful austerity of cold and remote lands.

Owls [abridged]

Late at night in the forest, who among hunters has not heard the strange sounds that once inspired such fear in timid folk who naively believed in some mysterious evil powers of nature? The frightening nocturnal sounds used to be attributed to secretive forest-dwelling beings such as warlocks and wood-demons. When the satanic laugh of the eagle-owl and the sinister hoots of other owls ring out through the dark forest, in the midnight hour an eerie feeling sometimes comes over even an experienced hunter. The fabled forest ogres which frightened our ancestors arise in the imagination. Often a weightless, winged shadow will flit soundlessly over the belated hunter's head in the darkness, and immediately vanish.

There are many enormous, tufted eagle-owls, and other kinds, great and small, dwelling in our forests. Some live in suburban parks, in orchards and old estates with old hollow lindens and oaks. Tawny owls will frequently take up residence in large, crowded cities, in old stone buildings and abandoned belfries.

It is unusual to see an owl by day. When surprised in its dark refuge, it will reluctantly fly out into the sunlight. Dazzled by the light, the bird of the night will perch clumsily, ruffling up its downy feathers, and sit quite still. Its huge, round eyes, which it helplessly closes, cannot bear the bright light. Its round, cat-like head rotates in all directions, as if on a ball-and-socket joint. When a human approaches, the bird clicks its bill menacingly and its feathers stir and rise.

Nocturnal owls are of much benefit to man. They kill rodents which cause damage to farms and forests. However, predatory owls also kill drowsy birds and even hunt at the leks of capercaillie and blackcock. Of the large owls, the eagle-owl is rightly considered the most rapacious. It is no wonder that diurnal birds detest it. If the feared nighttime robber should emerge into the light of day, birds big and small flock in from all sides, as if hearing some secret signal, to judge and punish their fierce enemy.

[...]

Some years ago I chanced to visit the Caucasus nature reserve. We stayed for a while in a remote mountain settlement surrounded by forest. The young zoologists who staffed the reserve had established a small menagerie. Besides some tame deer which roamed free, and a funny little bear cub, called Buka, who stole sugar from our table, there were bad-tempered wild cats and other small animals living in cages, and four owls in a large aviary of wire netting. During the day the owls perched on the boughs of a small dead tree in the enclosure, turning their round heads to observe the passers-by.

Our fourteen-year-old friend Vanya, the son of one of the foresters, looked after the owls. As other birds were scarce in the highland forest, he caught jays in small numbers to feed the owls. These jays were their only food.

It happened that Vanya fell ill and was unable to go hunting for a long time. For several days the owls were left with nothing to eat. The hungry birds went on sitting motionless on the boughs of their tree, apparently completely untroubled.

Early one morning, stepping down from the porch and stopping beside the aviary, I noticed to my surprise that it contained only three owls. The fourth had disappeared without a trace. I inspected the enclosure thoroughly. Apart from some old, dry pellets, there was nothing. I found no openings through which the fourth owl might have escaped.

Two days later there were only two owls left. There was no doubt: in the dark of night the hungry owls were killing and eating their companions. It was hard to imagine what happened at night in the aviary: no sign of any struggle could be seen, and there was not so much as a feather on the ground. (We know that, unlike diurnal raptors, owls devour their prey with all its feathers and small bones, which they then disgorge in little round pellets.) The living miscreants sat quietly, without stirring.

To put an end to the shocking "cannibalism," I suggested releasing the birds. On my advice, the door was left open overnight. In the morning the hungry owls were not there; they had flown out into the forest to hunt.

Imagine our surprise on the third or fourth day when we found the released birds back in the open aviary. They were sitting calmly on their dead tree, looking at us as before with their round eyes. After that we no longer shut the aviary, and every morning the owls would be in it. It was difficult to understand why they persisted in returning to the prison in which they had endured such cruel hunger.

The Director and the Books
(...of the Gogol Library in Rome)

Gaither Stewart

Pietro plunged the rusty key into the gaping keyhole of the library entrance door on the second floor of the palazzo on Rome's Piazza San Pantaleo. As each time he opened the ancient door of the Gogol Library, pride and a sense of proprietorship surged through his veins. In a way the key *was* the library itself. It was an old-fashioned key, long and heavy and twisted by age. In the semi-darkness of the hall way he had easily identified the key by touch among the half dozen others on the key ring. The Russian Gogol Library was named after the great Russian writer, Nikolai Gogol, who wrote his novel, *Dead Souls,* in Rome in the mid nineteenth century. The *Biblioteka imeni Gogolya* was now an institution in the Italian capital, designated in the telephone directory by that name. Pietro turned the key slowly, slowly, savoring the moment – both the feel of the famous key in his own pudgy white hands and the memory of the legend that the sculptor Antonio Canova had held the same key in his sensitive artist's hands to open the door to his studio over on Via delle Colonette. The Canova studio then became the first home of the Gogol Collection founded by Russian diplomats, artists and prominent émigrés who had fled to Rome after Russia's 1905 Revolution. Following the click after the first of the usual three turns of the key the nagging thought crossed Pietro's mind – as it did each day at the 11 AM opening – that he was in reality just a compromise "director" of the unique collection of Russian literature ... precisely because he was *not* Russian – he didn't have a drop of Russian blood in his veins – nor was he even a librarian. Furthermore – he thought after the second click – and the most incongruous of all the reasons for his nomination to his director status: his weak spoken Russian which excluded him from the eternal heated disputes plaguing the Gogol Library Board of Directors (GLBD) made up of withering and bickering old men who believed everything should and did remain the same. Everything under the sun. Nothing changed. The GLBD members personified the words of Ecclesiastes: *The thing that hath been, it is that which shall be; and that which is done is that which shall be done: and there is no new thing under the sun.* Ecclesiastes 1:9. What could Pietro Magari do against the GLBD chairman (self-proclaimed) who sixty years ago was a full professor at Rome University, Professor Sumashedtsov, an internationally recognized specialist in the unique curative qualities of the bark of the Siberian birch tree. At each of the frequent meetings he proclaimed his irrigation therapy theory that birch used with lots of fluids flushes out the urinary tract and purifies the blood and thus eliminates arthritis and many joint pains. After the third turn of the key, Pietro opened the door and stepped warily into his fragile realm. Fragile, but his.

In the same moment he entered the foyer he had the unpleasant recall of this morning's interview with a foreign journalist. Actually he had never been asked for an interview before. And he had no idea of how to handle it. Oh, well, he consoled himself, the typical Roman fatalist: the journalist will know what to do.

Now I, a foreign correspondent in the Italian capital, first got involved in the complex story of the Gogol Library as a journalistic assignment which quickly became an emotional involvement because of my love for Russian things since my three-year posting in Moscow ended last year in 1979 and I was sent to Rome. My Amsterdam newspaper's culture chief had heard about the existence of a lost collection of antique Russian books in Rome from our correspondent in Finland who saw a reference to "Gogol's lost books" in an Estonian émigré journal in Helsinki. So I was to follow up on this vague report from the most unreliable of sources: the émigré press. Notoriously, émigrés from any country and in any time and place either exaggerate or belittle everything in God's creation.

My first question to Pietro the Rock that morning was simple and to the point: How many volumes of Russian books does this collection contain?

"Collections!" he corrected me, true to GLBD tradition. "This library is made up of countless collections. But since *collections* here is misleading and there is no agreement as to what constitutes a volume, no real count has ever been accomplished. I *think* however there are a total of about 30,000 volumes, including many precious and priceless collector's books ... even first editions. Well, maybe there are 35,000. But maybe only 25,000. *Ecco la verità!*"

"So what about those countless collections. How many are there?"

"Actually, uh, first of all, I have some ideas that might surprise you. But that of course is neither here nor there. As my collector father said and wrote – my father collected everything, put them in fitting containers and then labeled them. In our cellar room at home where he kept his collections I once found a thick cloth sack with a stapled label: 'Bent nails; not to be used.' Uh, well, yes, I am straying. Collateral damage from my job. Uh, what was your question? Oh yes, numbers. If the truth be said, I truly don't know how many collections I, er, we, have either. Before I took over the directorship, the library consisted of ONLY private and personal collections … or so was claimed by members of the GLPD. I'll tell you a secret if you promise not to publish it. I think that back when the library was in the former Antonio Canova studio many Old Russian folks just sequestered – yes, they simply expropriated sections of books on the shelves and labeled them with their own name or the name of where their family originally came from. Like our famous *Kazanskaya kollektsiya*. It's really just a bunch of books, some literary, one geographical land survey … and a few scattered numbers of an old literary review published in Prague … or maybe it was in Sofia. Anyway, of before the 1905 revolution. The books had nothing to do with Kazan, but the grandparents of this old *gentleman*, hah,hah,hah, were from that faraway city. We have also the Riazan Collection, the Odessa Collection, and so on and so forth."

"So the reality remains that you don't know how many volumes the Gogol Library contains?"

Pietro pulled out of a drawer a folder containing stacks of papers with numbers and the names of collections scrawled across the top, or helter-skelter the room number and shelf designations. "Just take a look at this. Who can total the numbers? I can't. Neither can they …"

"They who?"

"The Russian board members, the GLBD. Nor does their English benefactor know how many volumes he is helping to preserve. He sends money every month to keep this library alive and every month asks the same questions you ask. How many volumes? He says he might have to come and count them himself. Good luck to him in that. If I had the …"

In that moment just when I thought we were getting somewhere, the old-fashioned telephone at Magari's desk squealed ... actually it groaned. Pietro stared at it, visibly perplexed: Should he answer? Who could be calling him ... except perhaps Sumashedtsov or some other crank from the GLBD?

"Well? Aren't you going to answer?"

"Huh? Oh yes, the telephone."

With two fingers he raised the receiver and held it a couple of centimeters from his ear. "Pronto!" he whispered. Then a long silence. I could hear the caller's voice from across the desk. A man was shouting in Russian. "*Da da,*" Pietro uttered, now sweating profusely. After more shouting in Russian on the other end, again Pietro's *da da. Da da. Da da.* Until finally he squeezed out a rather convincing "*ochen khorosho, Signor Uges* and hung up softly.

"Well, what a coincidence! Just as I was speaking of him. That was Langston Milford Uges, our benefactor from London. He speaks a little Russian, poor thing." Now back in his native language, Pietro becomes even more talkative. "He was married to a Russian lady named Lyudmila Zhukova who died a couple of years ago from cancer, *poverina.* Now I suspect – though I would never tell the GLBD this – I suspect he hopes to rename the library after her. You know, in the Russian way, *Biblioteka imeni Lyudmily Zhukovoy. Oh dio mio,* Sumashedtsov would go crazy and shoot himself ... or someone."

Like many Italians, Pietro was fascinated by the Anglo surname, Hughes. Though they are taught in school that English is not a phonetic language and is not pronounced as written, they find *Hughes* truly mysterious and in reality unpronounceable. Now since the letter h is silent in Italian, the capital H of Hughes is dropped a priori. So there remains this *ughes* to deal with – with another silent h – which is resolved in myriad ways. Some pronounce the name *ooze,* some *oose.* Others say UUUse. All eliminating that second h which resolves the hurdle of the impossible gh. Linguistic mysteries all. Pietro pronounced it *Uges,* with a hard g. I would later hear the more practical Russians of the GLBD call him simply Langston Milfordovich ... first name and patronymic.

"So anyway if you want to meet *Dottore* Uges, you should come back on Friday, the day after tomorrow, after eleven a.m."

"I will be here before noon to meet Langston ... I knew about him and his wife in Moscow when I was stationed there. You might not know that in Russia she was once a famous singer of popular music."

"Well, that indeed is interesting. Since you know that part of the story, I feel I should fill you in on the Gogol Library story ... things that Uges most likely does not know. You see, Doctor ..."

"Not Doctor, please. Signor, if you insist. Otherwise just call me Arrow ... or James. I'm James Arrow. People like that American Indian-sounding name and like to call me Arrow. *Freccia* in your language.

"Indian! Well! So now wait, what was I saying? Oh, yes. The mystery surrounding this institution. You see the Russians of the GLBD are terrified that without private financial support like today, the books and journals, the collections, the library itself will fall into Communist hands such as the Rome government or even worse the Slavistics Faculty at the University of Rome, which is where I hope it will eventually go. It is important that Mister Uges understand this. However, the GLBD which opposes name change anyway, would never, never agree to renaming it for a Soviet woman. *O Dio mio, no!* Why, they would rather burn it to cinders."

That Friday at around noon we met for the first time, though I felt as if I knew him anyway ... like in another life. Yet Langston Hughes-Uges was not as I'd expected at all. Youngish, an athletic type, average height, slim, and somewhat non-English in appearance, he had a special gleam in his eyes. Like that of an adventurer or a great game hunter or a sailor of faraway seas. Nonetheless I feared Langston was in for a great surprise when he encountered the board members of Pietro's fearful-fearsome GLBD, probably the most non-adventurous people in Old Rome.

"Pleasure to see you here, Arrow ... and to know that the Fourth Estate of the realm is interested in this project. A payback for my small contribution which is made in memory of my beloved wife who passed away some time ago. That's why I hope to keep the clergy and the nobility out of this ... in her memory, I mean."

"In any case, it's very generous of you, Langston. I'm somewhat involved in this story too. By the way I heard about your wife – and you also – when I was a correspondent in Moscow. So I know some of the story. Which I doubt the Library Board knows about."

Pietro, who didn't understand one word we were saying sat behind his desk and observed, a weak silly smile on his pink face. I imagine some of the thoughts running through his mind: he didn't want to risk his job and therefore he was for anything that guaranteed the continuation of Uges' financial support. On the other hand, the name change the Library benefactor had in mind would not further the solution he had aimed at from the start: transfer the whole *Biblioteka imeni Gogolya* – the name Gogol was an important selling point – to Rome University with Pietro Magari as its lifetime director.

But now the specter of Ludmila had appeared in Rome, flitting through the rooms of the palazzo housing the library and upsetting the Director's farsighted planning.

Now I too perceived a dilemma even if only the personal dilemma of the spectator rather than that of a participant. Obviously the hopes and desires of those involved were antithetical one to the other: Pietro, whose calculations were reflected in the constant changing of shape and coloring of his generally pinkish face wanted to keep his job forever under the aegis of some authority; the GLBD members wanted the Gogol Library to remain the Gogol Library, intact and independent of any secular or spiritual power, in a motionless and unchanging world. Langston wanted the library renamed for his beloved wife on which his future funding depended and it most likely mattered little to him whether the physical library was on Piazza San Pantaleo, in the old Canova studio, or in the labyrinthine halls of Rome State University. Though ethically I should have been more impartial, I felt a quickly formed allegiance to Langford because of our common backgrounds and love for the Russia we both knew.

At that point, as Pietro had warned me might happen, arrived noisily and unannounced Professor Sumashedtsov, generally known by his title and surname, a sign of special respect for the Chairman of the RLBD. The *ancien* Professor entered the Library's great room, full of vim and vigor, prepared to set things straight with this upstart Englishman. He'd thought it would be a cake walk to show this strange man who insisted on funding the Gogol Library that his role ended the moment he signed the monthly check to the Gogol Library Foundation, that fake institution whose role likewise ended the moment the check was magically transformed into Italian lira. So he was taken aback by the excellent Russian and the mundane, devil-may-care smile on the face of the mad dog Englishman.

So before Sumashedtsov could recover his faculties, Langston Milfordovich confirmed that he was in Rome to first count the library's volumes and secondly – upon which depended his participation in the Russian Library project – to legally change its name to *Biblioteka imeni Lyudmily Zhukovoy* in memory of his beloved wife.

"She now rests in Novodevichy Cemetery in her beloved Moscow, quite near to Gogol's remains ... and to the poet she loved, Vladimir Mayakovsky." Moscow, Novedevichy and now Mayakovsky!

Sumashedtsov's face had turned purple. His mouth open, his lower jaw dropped lower and lower. You could see he was choking, apoplectic as if near death itself; he was unable to utter a word for some ten long seconds after Langston, all aplomb and sang froid, had his say. When the professor recovered the quality of speech and his coloring began returning, he sputtered incomprehensible nonsense, then slowly turned toward the prestigious entrance door, the ancient wood of which he stroked with a tender gesture, as if saying goodbye to it forever.

Pietro was secretly gloating at the spectacle; he saw himself with his Russian library of countless invaluable volumes and with whatever name it would bear, installed in the University of Rome where he would grow old in peace without the GLBD breathing on his neck.

After a drawn out general silence Langston asked me to take him to my favorite restaurant in the area; we would celebrate. Celebrate exactly what was unclear to me. I had my story but nothing else. Langston and Pietro did have reason to celebrate. But Pietro said no, he had counting to do, so Langston Milfordovich and I sauntered to the door, the ancient wood of which I too caressed while hoping that Sumashedtsov hadn't already shot himself.

Emigration as a Dream

Yevsey Tseytlin

Translated from the Russian
by Veniamin Gushchin

Barely awake, I count the days. August – five, September – thirty ... This arithmetic gets old by the second month. I start counting weeks. Isn't that the way time is counted for kids – the not-yet- and just-recently-born? In four days, our three month "anniversary" of coming to Chicago. Still trying to figure out – is that considered a long time? (November 1996)

*

The pain is persistent. It comes back like contractions, bears in, gives no respite. Sometimes I just want to sink into it, adapt myself, go numb. But I can't. Of course, the pain is present in the night, but it feels farther away as I sleep. This pain has defined the month that I bid farewell to Lithuania and the month and a half I've spent in Chicago. The paramedics in Vilnius tried to help me, to no avail. In the States, generic painkillers from Walgreens finally beat the pain. As the wisemen say: The Almighty warns us through the language of pain.

*

The commonplace dimension of immigration is the English language. Our life is with it – and within it.

My English teacher is a Pole. He came to America as a child. Now he's thirty-seven. How do I know this? He told me himself. He also told me:

- about his wife, younger than him by five years, a doctor, who earns three times M's salary. A point of pride.

- about his lovers, "gyorlfrends," before he got married, his wife had been one of them for a few years.

- about his wife's likes and dislikes – she hates bad breath the most, loves to "make love"

- the reasons they fight; a common one : when M goes pee pee in the bathroom (the teacher says this in Russian), he lifts the seat up to avoid splash back; the wife comes home from work, hurriedly sits down directly on the cold bowl, jumps up, screams …

Sometimes I wonder: does M even have a wife? What if all of this is just a pedagogical technique to activate my understanding of his perfect English?

He sits in the middle of the room, legs stretched out. Without pausing his story, he can tie his shoelaces or scratch any part of his seal-like body in front of the whole class. As he talks, he checks the time inconspicuously. I checked many times: never a minute late, he cuts himself off, exactly at three:

"Break."

No, he doesn't half-ass his job – he's a true virtuoso. And, like any master of his craft, he enjoys when I tell him so.

"Oh, really?" M's false modesty.

His virtuosity is on full display at the start of the lesson. He sings songs, acts out different animals, different kinds of Americans … it would seem that M is also a virtuoso at hiding his perfect Russian.

Normally there are about ten or twelve people in the class. The desks were placed in a semi-circle. No textbooks, no grammar. Every day M. would pass around photocopied handouts. These were prompts. Imagine yourself a banker, deciding who to grant a loan to. Or a committee member, deciding, which school programs to cut, which to keep. Or … the handouts were raw data. "We'll discuss tomorrow."

At quarter-to-five sharp, M. shuts his mouth and leaves the room. On a cold day, he throws a brightly colored sweater over his shoulders. Just a short trip to his Toyota Camry in the parking lot.

I'll never know where he would drive off to. (January 1997)

*

"Interlude." That's the name of a Yuri Tynianov essay about Russian poetry in the 1920s. "Interlude" – I can't think of a better description for emigration. An emigrant is a man in an interlude.

*

Emigration or immigration? A useless debate. Any encyclopedia will tell you: an emigrant is someone who leaves their homeland; an immigrant – someone who moves to a different country. Why am I so interested in emigrants? Their fates inevitably harbor tragedy, or at least a melodrama. They've left Russia (or any other former Soviet republic) but haven't made it to America. They are in an interlude. Forever?

*

Emigrants themselves worry about justifying their emigration. They have used many different justifications over the years. Nowadays they typically address the "upper" as opposed to the "lower" person. No one will say or even think to themselves: "We are in exile; we are on a mission." One Chicago journalist in the early 2000s put it a lot more believable, with artless cynicism: "Take a piece of fresh Borodino bread, spread some Vologda butter on it, and stick a slice of Doktorskaya ham on top … you haven't forgotten your nostalgia for your homeland, have you?" (August 2005)

*

The great "truth-seeker" George Gurdjieff was certain: man is a machine. A being that lives mechanically but is submerged in the narcotic of dreams. Gurdjieff's experiments, dazzling and charming European intellectuals, pursued a single goal: awakening man from his "daytime dream."

Of course, emigration wakes up our sleeping conscience. I'll say! In the words of Dina Rubina, who never exaggerates, to emigrate "is to perform seppuku. And

91

your guts plop down on the sidewalk."

But emigration itself is also a dream.

*

Scientists happily declare: "Moving improves your memory. Over the course of their lives, people move an average of five times. Research shows that this is a difficult experience, even more difficult than divorce. However, scientists at the University of New Hampshire have found that moving has at least one upside. It helps you remember what has happened." (News agency in August 2016)

*

… As if disputing these scientific conclusions, an odd couple is slowly walking towards me on Devon Avenue. She is tall and lean, like a tree that has lost its leaves to fall. He is portly, unnaturally red-cheeked, barely reaching her shoulder. When they notice me from afar, they smile. Last fall in Hot Springs, Arkansas, we would go for frequent walks in the park, which seemed to hang over the city. Yuri had taught at university like me – fans would come into town just to hear his lectures. Now he was shy and silent. The most he had ever said to me, when we had just met, was: "You can call me by my first name, after all, we met in the West, where people don't use patronymics, isn't that so?"

It took me a while to realize that Alzheimer's had taken him a while ago. But he and his wife hid this fact masterfully. Fira would answer my questions about literature departments in Moldavia. Yuri would sadly and gently nod along.

Once when he dozed off on a park bench, drunk off the crisp mountain air, Fira told me their story in a whisper. Alzheimer's attacked her husband out of the blue and crushed him swiftly. *Thank God we were already here in Chicago, where the future isn't so scary. Thank God that he didn't get aggressive as the doctor warned. Thank God Yurochka didn't lose his intellect completely.* And he even came up with an explanation for his memory loss: "The majority of writers, bringing up the past, enliven it, take pleasure in remembering. But I don't want to remember. My past is soaked in sorrow."

92

*

"Emigration is an illness," I write in a notepad. And I forget about the most important thing: how long does the illness last? Of course, there are a couple options. Reading Frederick Perls, the founder of gestalt therapy, I come across his reminder: illness is an unresolved situation; it "can resolve through recovery, death or the restructuring of the organism."

*

Russophone communities in American cities become havens for the old. Mass emigration from Russia ended long ago. The old arguments in newspapers and on the radio are over: how many KGB agents came along with us? who really wrote *And Quiet Flows the Don*? was Georgy Zhukov Russia's savior or a butcher, heartlessly sending soldier to their deaths? Yesterday's debaters, who couldn't stand one another, now peacefully meet at the urologist's office, on a cruise to the Bahamas, or at an old folks' home. (December 2017)

*

Human destinies, submerged in the everyday, are revealed in emigration. Emigration highlights their brokenness, their strangeness, oftentimes their mystery.

*

On the very same Devon Avenue, the Chicago haven for Russian émigrés for many years, stands a man, pressed up to the wall of a grocery store. His appearance at once repels and attracts passersby. About himself he reports: I work as a beggar. It's hard to tell how old he is: somewhere between forty and sixty. In any case, I haven't seen any gray in his ragged bluish beard. He's got a prosthetic left leg, not covered by jeans as is often the case. His most notable feature are his eyes: big or at least they seem to be as he looks at you hard, intently, never averting his gaze.

We hadn't said a word to one another all these years. But I know his name: Ilyusha. A soft, warm name, as if poorly chosen for hire. Many American beggars hold out a can or a box with dollars, the clinking of coins reproaching passersby. But legless Ilyusha looks straight at you, piercing you with his gaze, and you take your wallet out without invitation.

One winter I saw Ilyusha at the doctor's. He recognized me as he was leaving and stopped. Confidently he asked, "Give me a lift to work?" It's only a five-minute drive, but walking is hard for Ilyusha: the wind in a Chicago winter stings and knocks over even the healthy. In the car he sits in silence, looking out the window – as if seeing the street he had spent decades on for the first time. Of course, Ilyusha wrinkles his nose at the bad smell from the gray coat he wears in any weather.

We got to talking: at some point he graduated from Moscow State University with a degree in philosophy. Philosophy? I raise a mental eyebrow. And I'm brought back to sentimental nineteenth century novels. I don't doubt this legend of émigré life, the kind that gets made into myth. But then T, who knows everything about everyone, swears that he really saw Ilyusha's diploma from Moscow State.

What brought him to Chicago and made him choose this ancient profession? I tried striking up a conversation with Ilyusha many times. But each time he would shove me away with his stare, closing like a bolt in the door.

*

Anatoly Simonovich Liberman, famous linguist, professor at the University of Minnesota, tells me over the phone:

"Our Soviet life averaged us out to a shocking extent. Generations like peas in a pod. As my wife would say, like a fireman's gray pants. We recognize each other instantly. All the same quotes, thoughts, memories.

And it's true: I recognize my people everywhere. I recognize my own fear in them without fail: most of us try to hide it. It's the only piece of baggage that, alas, an emigrant can't lose or leave in storage at the airport.

Fear is one of the main themes of my book *Long Conversations in Anticipation of a Joyous Death* (1996). For five years I have been listening to the confession of the dying Lithuanian Jewish dramaturg and critic j. These five years spent "on the very edge of life," j and I try to reconstruct his many fears and deal with them at long last. It just so happened that these fears found their resolution only in his death.

*

The day before yesterday after work I'm taking for a walk in the park near my house, talking on the phone. Suddenly – I hear a voice with a strong accent: "How nice – such beautiful Russian …" An older woman. I ask her: "Are you from Russia?" "No, from Latvia. I've been here almost thirty years. And I miss Russian terribly …" ?! "I really love learning languages. I know five already, now I'm learning my sixth – Japanese … I'm going to Japan soon for work placement." She tells me about herself some more. Nothing particularly notable, I can't quite figure out what she does for a living (something to do with non-traditional medicine) … We part ways after a few minutes. She asks to exchange phone numbers.

And soon she actually calls me, "I have a favor to ask of you. If we accidentally meet in some public place, pretend that you don't know me …" She repeats this a few times. I calm her down, give her my word to keep quiet, don't question anything she says. I don't want to get deep *inside* her fears.

*

At one point I started recording the dreams of Jews. I began from the Exodus from the country of the red pharaohs. A million people disappeared, as if they had evaporated in history and time. I thought: it was through dreams that I could understand the tragic and tangled history of the Soviet Jewry. No matter how many times we tried to read it today, much remains only a conjecture. Maybe our dreams, I thought, could clarify something. Something that people couldn't talk about before. Something they had already forgotten. And something that they hide to this day – even from themselves (some of these notes made into my book *The Aftertaste of Dreams*, 2012).

What about the dreams of emigrants? Here are the ones that repeat, the ones that psychologists assure us are the most important: "We're sitting in airplane, just touched down in New York. The adults are disgruntled, the children are crying. Finally, thank god, everything got resolved." About ten people have told me this exact "nightmare" with only slight variations.

*

An interview with some emigrants-insomniacs: you wake up at 3 AM and can't fall back asleep until the morning. They say that at these times the heavens are trying to tell you something important.

Another typical answer: "I love lying in the dark with my eyes closed. I'm trying to see myself from the outside. For years I've been treating myself as a stranger. I ask myself: is there some purpose to this person's life? Is this his fate?"

*

I've been editing a Russophone monthly publication in Chicago for more than twenty years. There is no shortage of this kind of publication in the States: something between a newspaper and a journal. I could write a book about "my time as editor." It's a shame that this book already exists (see Mark Twain's notes or the novellas of Dina Rubina).

*

Emails from William F. are full of surprises. He is also a "philosopher," one of the many "philosophers" of the Russophone community. His ideas always shock me. Here's his missive from today, which he clearly wrote to provoke a response from the editors:

"It is known that are many lesbians and homosexuals in our society. Typically, they don't have kids. However, you shouldn't mismanage your own biological material. Why shouldn't we support bisexuals impregnating lesbians? That way these women would achieve harmony in their lives. And we'll be sure to get major population growth. Indeed, homosexuals need to be slowly, but surely – with the help of scientific advancements – be led into the ranks of bisexuals." (November 6, 2017)

96

*

In the new edition of Yuri Olesha's diaries, which was previously called "Not a day without dropping a line," now reedited and expanded as *The Book of Farewell*, I read: "Human fate, lonely human fate (…) is an avoidable subject for generations. Works of world literature are based upon it. The best thing written about this in the last few years – Remarque's book. It somehow echoes with a different book of solitary human fate – Hamsun's "Hunger." Now I turn to my own fate and I saw: loneliness. In this epoch of mass movements let there be a book about loneliness.

Loneliness, like falseness, is the symbol of emigration. (August 2000)

*

I come into the editorial office at different times – at 9, 10, 11 AM. There's no rush: I could work from home. But Boris is sitting in the waiting room, restless. I'm ashamed, I apologize profusely before him every time. But what's there to apologize for: in America you set up a meeting beforehand, no one "drops in" like in Russia.

"What's new?" I ask, though I already know his response, "Sorry, I don't get enough communication." Boris is a pretty good poet. I ask him to read me his old poems, ask him about Tajikistan, where he lived and was published some time ago. What else can I do for him?

*

These old emigrants (eighty and over) are the typical Soviet crowd. They rarely come to insight like Boris, who concludes his letter with a sigh: "Communism is a wonderful idea! We just have to make sure it never comes true."

*

Another point of discussion about emigration: "Are you happy in the US?" Svetlana P is indignant: "I didn't come here and learn English just to clean other people's home …" Inna M responds, "Svetlana would be right, of course, if she didn't speak English like so many of our old folks: Yours mine yesterday coming …"

We love to overestimate *our own*.

*

Books rush into the publishing house on a stream. I'm often puzzled: why do so many, having just emigrated, want to be become writers? And – immediately pick up "quill and ink," that is to say they learn how to work the computer.

Here they lose their profession (typically, it's become redundant). But in their soul they feel the an unshakable urge: I have a unique life experience, I absolutely must talk about it.

Alas, writing books is also a profession. 99.9% of books written in emigration are the colorless products of graphomania.

*

Emigration as an idea and as a reality are two different things.

As an idea, emigration is wonderful: it shows the writer the essence of many things, especially his true calling.

Alas, the reality of emigration is different. Crude. Cynical. Harsh. All highlighting the uselessness of creative work.

*

The Russian writer, of course, is among the emigrants. It makes no difference if he knows English. He thinks and writes in Russian.

He is in the interlude. Isn't that why so many writers in emigration are overwhelmed by anxiety and frustration? Frustration at whom? At Russia, where they weren't appreciated and even now the critics don't notice them. At antisemites (back in Russia, though there's no state anti-Semitism there anymore). At American bureaucrats. And of course, at themselves. At their own fate. Sooner or later they understand the purposelessness of this feeling. Is it submission or are they only pretending?

The essence of this feeling was formulated by Fritz Perls: anxiety is the rupture, the tension between "now" and "then."

*

The talented poetess Anna B. passed away. Her articles about émigré writers are full of spite. Boomerang? How did she not understand that? Of course, she understood. But it was too late. On her death bed, she would call up the people that just recently she had doused with buckets of bile. Now she asked for their forgiveness.

*

"Hello, brother, it is very hard to write!" the Serapion Brothers would say to one another. In emigration, this greeting comes off mocking: who's going to hear the lonely voice of the author, trying to say something in a foreign language?

Still emigration is the best place for creative work. That is to say if you're able to rein in your irrepressible vanity.

*

In November 2013 an old doctor died in Chicago, an emigrant from Ukraine, Roman Vershgub. So many people take a secret with themselves when they die. I always thought that there's no need to try to figure it out – everyone has the right to leave some act in your life-plot unspoken. But nevertheless, this was a special case.

I heard that Roman Vershgub writes short stories from Efim Petrovich Chepovetsky, the famous children's poet, who had spent his last years living in Chicago.

"Remarkable prose," Efim exclaimed, "The only issue is that Roman doesn't want to publish any of it."

He typed out his stories on a typewriter, making two-three copies. And he give them to two-three people to read. When we met, Roman granted me this honor. What grabbed me about his stories? They were clearly written by a professional.

I made the same mistake as the others. I asked him, I can recommend your works to one of the émigré journals that I'm a part of, if you want? He gave a hard pass.

He was already hopelessly sick by then, and he knew that. So eventually he caved to his friends and started reading his stories in Chepovetsky's literary studio. However, he was even more adamant in his belief in the uselessness of publication. Maya, Roman's widow, went against his wishes. I can't criticize her though. In the past legends about Maya the homeopath would travel around Kyiv. Now, a few decades later, she did Western gymnastics, drove a car. She came into my publishing house a few times. She was looking for advice: how do I make the collection? What should I call the book? And the most important thing: how do I interpret the subtext of this or that short story.

She was troubled by the mystery of her husband. Roman never let his wife read his prose. Was he shy, knowing her good taste and harsh judgments? Maybe. Did he not trust her? Doubtful. There was point denying: he loved Maya and was dedicated to her for the many years of their marriage.

I had collected a big folder of Vershgub's stories. Sometimes I look them over. These are sad stories, entirely cheerless at first glance. One of them has following epigraph: "Successes are illusory, troubles are real." The hero of this novella is a young scientist named Vitaly, who deserves the title of genius. All of a sudden he abandons his dissertation at the defense, leaves his parent's home – moves in with an unattractive women, a lot older than him ("mama's boy"). Sasha the surgeon who performs impossible procedures suddenly loses his touches and desperately tries to figure out, who's fault is it – is it really him? ("made his own luck"). "I recognize real events and real people in his stories," Maya tells me. And finally I get it: the space of R.V. stories is a kind of psychoanalytic laboratory. Here he as someone who doesn't believe in God but trusts fate aims to get into logic and meaning, or that the illogic and meaninglessness of being.

In early April I bumped into Maya, again on Devon. We hurriedly exchanged new. "Did you get the book?" "Not yet. It came out already? Congratulations! How many copies?" "Fifty." "That's so few …" "It's a lot. Thirty books are lying around in the closet – nobody needs them."

Maya sighed: "Up there, in the sky, Roman is judging me, of course …"

*

In the US there are more than two million registered authors. Sometimes thinking about this makes me not want to write. I imagine the competition between two million ants.

*

But still, to defend creative work. Man was made in God's image. How's that relevant? Man was – first and foremost – created by a demiurge. Creativity helps the emigrant to keep within himself a thin, constantly shrinking layer of spirituality.

*

The tragedy of emigration: it gives freedom; however, frequently it closes the world off instead of opening it up.

"What should I do with my freedom?" The same Efim Petrovich Chepovetsky asks me this. He's over ninety years old. But he still writes, loves getting together. At one point his poetry was praised by Samuil Marshak, Lev Kassil, Mikhail Svetlov. Millions of children would read his books, their names spring to mind: "Mytsik the Mouse," "Fidget, Crumbling, and Notso," "About the Great Queen Nasturtium Petrovna," "The Soldier Peshkin and Company" … I met Chepovetsky more than forty years ago, when I wrote my first book about the "school of Vsevolod Ivanov." This trailblazer of the Russian avant-garde of the 1920s, the oppositional classical author of Soviet literature taught young writer first and foremost about artistic searching, constant doubt, which is so important in art. In February 1972 I published previously unknown reviews of Ivanov about the "younger generation" in *Literaturnaya Gazeta*. The most interesting review was dedicated to the work of Efim Chepovetsky. Now, forty years later, EP persistently keeps on asking me: "So what do I do with my freedom?"

*

Mikhail K. died – a somber man. He helped so many and never expected thanks in return. And it seems like he never got it. No one really knew his life story. M himself would tell me: during the war he was in recon, ended in the camps (in Stalin's). After being released, he quickly tried to compensate for what he had missed, went to university, quickly defended his dissertation, became famous for his inventions, which was the reason they didn't let him out into the West for so long. As he was telling me his story, one minor detail bothered me: at the start of the war M was very young, but still he managed – all so quickly? – to get the rank of colonel, which he didn't get back after his rehabilitation. MK's American fate was obvious: he became a university professor, had his own grad students, started his own company.

In his huge apartment, filled with antiques, M looks like a weary traveler who accidently stumbled into an expensive hotel. As if nonchalantly, without giving much meaning to his confession, he remarks, "I have no one to talk to. I don't watch TV. I only read the news in the papers. Everything is clear to me anyway."

Three times a week, without fail, M visited the nursing home, one of these days, the oncology division of Lutheran General Hospital. He told me about his visits, unperturbed and precise as always, "They're just lying there, nobody needs them, their kids have forgotten them. My only comfort is that they would be a lot worse off back in Russia"; "When they need me, I translate from English, Russian, Yiddish …"; "I always read them Scripture. They listen intently, though they probably don't understand much."

M had his own relationship with the Bible. He was always unafraid and unequivocal:

"The Torah was given to us by aliens. Every reasonable person knows this. Aliens are the representatives of High reason. They are the ones who gave Earth moral laws for humans to live by. How could it be otherwise?"

He would look at me inquisitively, with a mischievous glint in his eyes, as if inviting a discussion about the Revelation at Sinai. Of course, I didn't try to argue with MK.

*

My oldest friend, the wonderful writer Vladimir Ilyich Porudominsky tells me about Cologne, where he's been living for eleven years: "I like it here, but this city will be never become my past. It doesn't grow into me, only out." V.I. left Moscow for Germany, following the families of his two daughters. He left the same room he was born in seventy-seven years ago. (May 15, 2005)

*

September 11, 2001. Las Vegas. We were going to meet up with my university friend Emil Gorshteyn and his wife Dina. The night before, September 10 – a wonderful evening, the four of us. In the morning – a call from Emil: "Turn on the TV."

I see the Twin Towers fall in New York, thinking to myself: what is this? Is this really the end of civilization?

Walking out of our hotel room, we walk through casino hall. There – everywhere – huge TV screen that no one is paying attention to. The game goes on. (September 18, 2001)

*

"… So, a waking dream," I ask again, happy that I have solved the riddle of emigration, "What is that?"

Efraim B. gives an inspired speech about the *galut*. The exile of the Jews for thousands of years, which our wisemen call a *dream*.

—

"When will the Lord return the children of Sinai from captivity, [all that has happened] will appear to be a dream." *This was the song sung to the Levites as they stood at the steps of the Temple.*

—

Why is the *galut* a dream? Contradictory phenomena come together here. Lies suddenly take the form of truth. Reason is eclipsed (the Hassidim believe that this is a dream too).

George Gurdjieff spent long years thinking about this, persistently trying to convince his student of this truth that was so apparent to him.

*

It turns out that my notebooks have long been filled with waking dreams, or people from dreams, to be precise.

*

The professions emigrants take up are surprising. Moti Sh. Tells me about his friend Borya (another undocumented immigrant, just left Chicago for New York):

"What do you think, what kind of jobs did they offer to Borya? Selling shoes for dogs! Not in some small shop, mind you, but on a big plaza ..."

Moti is Israeli. Shaved head, blue, mischievous eyes. I think he's impossible to confuse, though Moti often tries to confuse the people he's speaking to with the shameless look in his eyes. He was born and went to school in Moscow, moved to Israel, got his bachelor's at the Hebrew University of Jerusalem in political science, speaks three languages – Russian, Hebrew, and English. He became undocumented in Chicago after his student visa application got rejected. His life consists of his neglected apartment, a few neighbors, roommates, random side-jobs. Why doesn't he go to Israel or Russia? Moti won't answer this question. He likes this condition of eternal indeterminacy, of complete openness to fate. Moti talks about his last job with gusto. He drives around a doctor who makes house visits to the elders (this isn't really a common thing in the US). While the doctor is talking to his patient, Moti lounges in his car, smiling at his own thoughts, mentally shuffling his options for the future.

*

I call him up and – he comes over. Calm, serious. He paces my apartment with a tape measure and calculator. He's not worried about the particularities of our refurbishments: my wife and I want to paint the walls and the ceilings, but instead, crushed by fatigue, decide not to move the cabinets, nor to take the books off the shelves, nor to put dishes and papers away in boxes. "Let's call it a cosmetic refurbishing," says Sergey with a smile, understanding everything. He talks to me without fawning, but also without that barely concealed boorishness, the sin of many Russian handymen. He names a price a bit higher than what I was planning on paying. But I don't argue with him, I'm already sure: he's our guy, he's one of our own.

Sergei works quietly, rarely asking me questions. I'm sitting with my laptop in the kitchen, which was painted last year, making the next edition of the journal. At midday I find the lunch my wife made in the fridge and invite Sergei to join me at the table. He declines and takes his own food out of his blue bag. He does agree to join me for tea with candies. At tea, he calmly tells me that he's in the country illegally. Of course, I get the logic of his bravery: in America no one is going to arrest you for confessing this to them, at least not yet, and perhaps I could help him.

I look Sergei over furtively, doing the mental math: he's thirty-five, he's spent eight years in Chicago. His hair is the color of wheat, always neatly cut; his eyes small, but always warm, tiger-colored. He has a straight nose, big hands, which, I have come to believe, are capable of doing anything. His clothes aren't quite working-class, he dresses as if he's counting on being seen by someone whose opinion means a lot to him: his jeans, his gray flannel shirt have been fitted to his form. It's amazing how put together, elegant even Sergei remains by the end of the day.

What's so magnetizing about him to me? It's his calmness, or more accurately his feeling of freedom, which I can't quite understand. It would seem that Sergei has to hurry back to Russia, hurry to live his life, not just get ready for it. His wife Anya, kids – a boy and a girl – are back in the suburbs of Tambov. He's got no future in America, and yet he's still breathing easy. He sends money through Western Union once a month and shows me a photo of a two-story house, built on his blueprint. And is completely silent about leaving.

Sometimes I really want to see Sergei. I am able to find reasons. The door to the entranceway closet breaks, a rocking chair made in China breaks into pieces. He fixes everything well and quickly. Then we eat breakfast (or lunch) and talk *life.* Sergei refuses to take my money. We're mates now, if not bosom friends. But I always make sure to sneak a few bills into his coat pocket as he leaves. And he accepts, defeated by my reasoning: "If you don't accept, I won't be able to call you up the next time."

Of course, soon I learn the reason behind his illogical optimism. "I have to introduce to Rita sometime," say Sergei. They both live in the so-called Ukrainian Village in a house with four apartments. Each has their own apartment to be sure, but they're together. Six years already. No more about Rita. Though Sergei tells me about his communes of undocumented immigrants. "I'm something like their village elder." I'm quick to imagine their frequent parties, night and day ("we're around fifteen"), their unsentimental care for one another, which keeps them alive: undocumented immigrants, for example, have a tough time accessing health care. Their sad farewell: now and again someone books a one-way ticket, though they can't imagine life outside this strange wilderness.

—

"What do you do on Sundays," I ask him once, when Sergei comes on a Monday. Somehow, I get the feeling that he wanted me to ask him this.

Nevertheless, he's embarrassed, he even blushes: "We spend the whole day in bed. And we don't get tired at all." His eyes light up – a typical, funny kind of masculine pride. "And you know sometimes when I wake up I forget where I am. And then I think that we are still in our village, that first happy year after my marriage to my wife."

—

I never ended up meeting Rita. I catch a glimpse of her in August in a video on Sergei's phone. She'll tell him about leaving the day before her flight. "She couldn't do it earlier. She hadn't made up her mind. And I don't blame her. Her eldest son is getting married in Kaliningrad." She gets on board the plane without looking back. Petite, as if frozen, in a fashionable summer outfit, very attractive even in her hopeless despair. (December 2016)

*

The joy of oblivion. The topic of an essay that I've been trying to write for years before I realize that this thought has become obvious to everyone.

As everyone knows, the acceptance of death, agreement with it is one of the stages on man's final journey. But it turns out that it's possible to accept one's own oblivion just as peacefully. And even achieve a joyful state.

… On Thursday Yura and Fira come to visit me. They are flustered and calm – all at once. They want to tell me about a recent, unusual decision of theirs. "You know," says Fira, "in the late '70s the KGB would bring Yurocka in for questioning. Yes, as an anti-Soviet dissident. Then everything seemed to quiet down and fall into place. But so many of Yurochka's manuscripts that were seized by the authorities, and we never got them back. So imagine: just recently a young research from Moldovia got in contact with us. And told us the most unbelievable news! He found one of Yura's plays in the archives of the KGB. What play, you ask? Scenes from life in Ancient Rome. But it's full of allusions to contemporary issues, like all liberal literature of the time. *The play's a work of genius! the young man tells us on the phone, You must publish it!* And he seemed to have already gotten in touch with a press that was compiling a volume. We're completely flustered. Yurochka is adamant that he's never written a play in his life. I wasn't with him back then. Maybe there's been some kind of mistake? Maybe it's KGB setup? In any case, we decided to decline the offer to publish. Why? Would it even change our lives?"

From my window I can see them walking on Devon Avenue, not in a hurry as always. Yura, as if he's a child again, is afraid to let go of his wife's hand. And the great joy of oblivion, consciously chosen and accepted within their souls, makes them happy.

*

So many resent that profane banality that is ever-present in emigration. But this banality is the only unshifting ground of emigration.

*

A Russian restaurant with a characteristically pretentious name Zhivago was set up near a graveyard. The restaurant is always full of costumers: after funerals people come here – *to commemorate*. I like that. Remembering the dead, you think of yourself, of course. Your life is short, my dear. What have you done, what have you accomplished? You've tried to get ahead, lied your way through. You've buried your talent so deep that you won't find it. Ahead of you, ahead of everyone is a hole in the ground, surrounded by cement tiles. But a foul joy defeats all of these thoughts with a shot of vodka: you're still alive, alive!

*

I always feel bad for Russian doctors in America. Their path is predetermined and difficult. They come here with the degrees with Russian medical institutes when they're already over forty. They have to pass their exams – in English, of course – to get their degree recognized. Then spend a few years in residency (and it's tough to get in!). And they still need time to end up millionaires.

*

"And your books plop down on the sidewalk," writes Dina Rubina about the first days of emigration. In late August and in September of 1996 the Chicago sidewalk is melting from the heat. Our past life falls away into thin air without a trace – as if it never happened. But our new life still hasn't begun …

Everything is the same for everyone. "Depression climbs aboard with a measured pace. The world goes dark." That's Olga G. Though now she shares her jo with me: " … right now, it's as if I've been born again. As if the bag over my head has been lifted." (May 1, 2007). For long how though?

*

Sasha G. is honest with me: "I sing while I'm driving. Strangely enough, it's always the same two songs. Yuz Aleshkovsky's "Cigarette Butt" and "Hey, man, raise your collar …" I even sing when I'm driving with my wife. She gets annoyed: the same two songs, year after year." Has anyone considered how songs about the prison camps are a kind of therapy for emigrants? In moments of utter anguish, I often reread Varlam Shalamov's most depressing stories.

*

Is emigration a dream? You open your eyes, and there's nothing left. How little is left of Russian émigré literature from the 1920s-30s. We've only heard about the brightest names, many of which were famous even before the Revolution. And how many young talented voices remained unheard. Their works are mentioned as bitter reminders in the letters and diary entries of others. I've discussed this with the literary scholar Olga Korosteleva. He accomplished a miracle: doing the work of an entire institute, he reconstructed the life of the literary emigration in the '20s and '30s. Nevertheless, the gaps in our literary memory are vast, often irreversible. One of the naïve question that I ask Korosteleva: what can we do so that this never happens again? (See our conversation in the journal *Seagull*, June 10, 2016.)

*

Fifteen minutes before the Russian bookstore closes, an old lady appears at the door. She wears a white panama hat on her head (a greeting from her pioneer childhood). She carries in her hand a big wallet made of straw, the same one my grandmother used to take to the market. This is clearly not the old lady's first visit to the store: she immediately comes to the shelf with books on esoterica. She's looking for something very intently, hurriedly scanning all the tables of contents.

"Can I help you with anything?" asks the saleswoman.

"No, I got it," the old lady is adamant. But then she looks up at the clock and realizing that she's come too late and that she'll have to ask for help, says: "I need a book about how to change fate."

Funny? Doubtful. Again, a typical emigrant theme – changing your fate (2008 April)

*

Answering the interview questions from a German magazine *Kreschatik*, which had its anniversary in 2017, I suddenly remember how surprised and happy I was to find twenty-one Russian-language bookstores when I had just moved to Chicago. Five of them were located very close to my house. Oddly enough each store had its own face. One of them exclusively sold new books, fresh off the plane from Moscow. The owner of another store, a graduate of the Literary Institute, without any considerations of profit, ordered Russian and translated literature that had an experimental vibe. A third drew me in with monographs about art history, albums of artist copies. However, I am certain: the most amazing was a store called the House of the Russian Book. Amid their paintings and engravings, collected works, and many rare editions I could always find something unexpected. And the hospitable owner of this festive kingdom, Ilya Rudyak, a writer and director from Odessa, would talk passionately about almost every book, like he was reading poetry. You only had to ask. I would often drop by for Ilya: to talk, to breathe in that special air – no, not of book dust, but the air of Russian culture. By the way, Yevgeny Yevtushenko, a great bibliophile himself, loved to come here.

... all of these stores have long gone out of business. Their owners, mostly naïve idealists, would go broke. Now there are three kiosks in Chicago that still sell books in Russian: one found its place in a Russian deli, the other two in Russian drugstores.

Of course, American bookstores also constantly go out of business. These multi-story palaces where you often come and spend the whole day. You can not only browse books and magazines to purchase but also sit down and read them. You can also grab a cup of coffee with your friends, even a bite to eat. And again set sail across the sea of books. It's just that there are fewer and fewer seafarers.

Leaving for America, it was painful to bid farewell to my personal library, which I had collected for twenty years with a passion I couldn't quite understand myself. Many shared my feelings. And now it's the Reader that we're biding farewell to. He is going away with frightening speed. And more often it seems that emigrant publications are read only by their own authors.

*

An invasion of fortunetellers, clairvoyants, ancestral sorcerers. The Siberian shaman Ayun-batyr cures infertility in individual seances. The contactee Bonifaty changes your fate … my friend MK once paid a visit to a contactee. "He help you?" "So much! And I'm lucky: I bought the privilege of contacting Bonifaty at any time without a line. I can call him, get his advice on any difficult situation in my life."

"And how much did it cost?" MK hesitates, doesn't want to say – moreover, that's not what people do in the West. But then she remembers that we're friends. And spills: "Five thousand."

MK didn't inherit her money. I sincerely admire this stout, aged, but still beautiful woman for her valiant resistance to emigration. She came to America at age fifty. No English. With a seriously ill husband and two teenage daughters. One time she explained to me: "One daughter is from a previous marriage, the other from this one; my husband died in a year, I had to do something quick …" Like many others, she chose to clean apartments. She was learning English at the time, picked up driving a car, passed the exam that confirmed her qualifications as a lab chemist (though in a past life, she was a research chemist, the head of a big lab), counted every dollar, paid for her daughters' college, bought a good apartment.

MK is not an idiot. But she is lonely: her daughters have their lives. Then she got diagnosed with cancer. So she had a choice: go into surgery or wait. The contactee – a sweet young man with a decisive gaze – gave the advice MK wanted to hear: wait. After consulting the doctors, MK decides to go for the surgery. "Do you still talk with Bonifaty," I ask a few months later. "He's hard to get a hold of," MK says without judgment. Maybe she's says so still thinking about some higher power that will intervene in her life.

*

On the cover of the Chicago Russian community weekly is a portrait of a priest in church garb. His words in quotes jump out at you: "I beg forgiveness from every one!" Mikhail Ts., a priest at the Apostle Orthodox church gives an interview. In which he fervently repents for his sins. Back in Kyiv in 1978 he dreamed of becoming a priest, but instead became a KGB agent. M. Ts. chose his own pseudonym

– Athos. (This pseudonym was not chosen at random: the future Father was an accomplished fencer). Having parted ways with the KGB and arrived in the US, M. Ts. felt a different calling for himself. He started making international driver's licenses for undocumented Mexican immigrants. But one day "the special forces turned up out of the blue and called me nearly the godfather of the Russian mafia in Chicago ... I got out on bail, but with probation." All of this was long ago, twenty year ago. Still his voice is shaking: " ... today I beg forgiveness from everyone for my sins and mistakes." But no, there's more. M. Ts. ends by giving gift to his readers: "In Chicago I am the only priest who will, given our "military situation," hear confessions over the phone ... completely free of charge, of course." (April 2018)

∗

Do you anticipate your own death? The answer is obvious. A flood of stories come to mind. But I'll stick to telling just one, my own.

Like everyone, I had heard many times about the robberies in the "disadvantaged" areas of Chicago. The advice of seasoned veterans: never under any circumstance should you argue, run away, resist, or call for help ... You should give everything you can, everything they ask for. The best advice: keep some bills in your pocket (what if it's a drug addict in altered state that attacks? He will shoot or beat you up without a second thought).

The other Saturday I'm walking home from the synagogue around 1 PM. It was raining in the morning, but now it's dry and a bit frosty. As I'm walking, I start thinking to myself: "There you go, life has passed me by ... No, not like that ... The vagueness of my boyhood and youth is gone. Everything ahead is crystal clear. The only thing left to know: what's the end going to be like and when will it come ..."

They say when souls descend into this world in order to take on bodily form, the exact date of our departure is already set. So is our mission for coming here. Suddenly, the Almighty gives you choice: you control the route of your earthly life. But the final date cannot be changed.

Such banal thoughts ...

My walk back home takes about fifteen minutes. Suddenly from one of the alleys (near a construction site where they're raising modest two-million-dollar mansions) two boys run out to catch up with me. They are African American, look to be around eighteen years old, well-dressed. One of them overtakes me, stretches out his hand: "Good Shabbos!"

Then sudden he switches into a menacing tone: "Give us your money … quick … or I'll start shooting."

His hand drops into his pocket, gets out a pistol, then hides it again, pointing the barrel at me through his coat.

Why am I so calm? Maybe because I am remembering my own thoughts from a few minutes ago. Could it be that the Almighty had prepared me for this kind of death?

"I don't have any money." It's true. On the Sabbath, Jews aren't supposed to carry around any cash.

The boys look at one another. The street is still empty.

"I'm going to count to three … one … two …"

He counts to eight. And I'm waiting for the shot. Could this really be? Is this it?

As someone has given me a hint, I take off my new Italian coat:

"This is for you!"

Finally understanding that I really have no money on me and totally ignoring my coat, they turn around and walk away.

—

Four days later this still looks quite strange.

It's strange: on the Sabbath in our largely Orthodox Jewish neighborhood there were no pedestrians on the street (the synagogues had just finished their services). It's strange that the boys had appeared here. And that they had disappeared silently.

—

Was that a rehearsal of the departure or just a daytime dream?

2018

Hostile Territory

Lena Wolf

When I was at school my favorite subject was target shooting. I enjoyed both handgun and rifle shooting. I did enjoy grenade throwing as well, however due to my slightly shorter size, the second smallest in the class, I could never quite get the mandatory 25-meter throw no matter how hard I trained. Target shooting was a different story and my height in this case seemed to work to my advantage. I spent hours training and by the end of that first year I was fast, I was accurate, and I was deadly.

The basic military training at school started when we were fourteen and our teacher, Sergey Sergeevich, had only recently come to Kazakhstan and was new to our school. He was a proud member of the Communist Party, our only party, and described himself as a Soviet patriot. This was not unusual as we all wanted to grow up to become Party members and we were all proud patriots. Both his father and grandfather fought fascist Germany in the Second World War and both of them gave their lives for the country. And nothing less was expected of us, when the right time came.

The basic military training lessons always took place in the reinforced bunker in the cellar of our school building unless we did grenade throwing, which was always outside on the athletic track field. The reinforced bunker was there in case the Americans declared nuclear war on our country and the bunker would be the place where we, the pupils of the school, would survive to then go on and fight for our country. We all knew that if the nuclear attack happened some of our parents would not survive unless there was a bunker at their workplace as well. In my case I was lucky. My mum's job was to manage a team of economists at the sports city – a city within a city, and apart from having great training facilities to train future Soviet athletes to make our country proud, it also had its own school, its own shop, a *stolovaya* (a utilitarian canteen), and a bunker. And in my dad's case, he was a long-distance bus driver in Kazakhstan. I mean a really long-distance driver. Like

Kazakhstan long-distance. Each job took him 2000 kilometers away, and sometimes all the way to Russia and to Siberia. I imagined him driving far to the east of Kazakhstan, to the magnificent Tien Shan mountains – our part of Kazakhstan was more flat – which would offer him much needed protection from the nuclear radiation so he could survive, join other survivors, and be ready to fight. I was lucky and I was prepared.

One of the first lessons that we did with Sergey Sergeevich was first aid and how to bandage various types of injuries. We covered a hand injury, a bullet wound to the shoulder, a broken leg, and a head injury from a grenade splinter. I volunteered to be the person with the forehead injury. I thought it was possibly the most difficult one to treat and maybe also the most patriotic one because it would bleed a lot. And as I walked up to the blackboard where the bandaging instructions took place, I imagined myself to be someone who had just saved a mother and a child or an elderly person from a certain death by risking my own life. We needed a second volunteer to do the bandaging of my head and I could see my friend Oksana slowly raising her hand but then putting it down again as someone in the class asked Sergey Sergeevich whether they should help a German if the war really happened?

"And what do we do if there are several other injured people like a fellow Russian or a Ukrainian?"

"Or a Kazakh?" someone shouted.

"Is it not our duty to help a fellow Russian first before helping a German?"

All of us looked at Sergey Sergeevich, expecting an answer, but he remained silent. He was not a man of many words, nor was he a man of action. But he firmly believed that every single situation is preparation for the imminent war. And so it was for us to sort it out without anyone's help. He did not say that in words, but we all understood it.

We should help a fellow Russian first, the class agreed. "I only got the head injury because I risked my own life to save someone," I told them. "And besides, am bleeding to death here while you are talking down there. And there is nobody else who is injured. Is it not your duty to help the injured?"

But the discussion continued as they analyzed the order in which the injured should be helped. First, they would help any injured from the Soviet republics. They discussed whether all Soviet nationalities should be equal in getting first aid and they agreed that yes, a fellow Kazakh or Uzbek and fellow Russian will have the same first-aid status because all nationalities within the Soviet Union are equal. Also, this was more practical as they would not need to ask for a passport every time before giving first aid. The next would be fellow communist countries like Poland and China, Mongolia and Cuba, just to name a few, as they would be in the war as well, fighting alongside the Soviet Union to defend communism. I looked at the Polish kid in our class. He was looking down at his desk, not engaging. He was safe.

They continued by clarifying that they would help a German if the German was from the Democratic Republic of Germany.

"Which Germany are you from?" they asked me.

"From the Kazakh one," I told them. "I grew up here."

"But you weren't born here, right?!"

"It doesn't matter" I told them, "I would be fighting for our county and, being the best in our class, would probably be saving all your lives."

As there were no volunteers, Sergey Sergeevich suggested I should do the bandaging myself. The instructions were very clear and all I had to do was to follow them. I bent my head down slightly and took the bandage in both hands and then wrapped it tightly around my forehead. Doing it tightly was important to stop any potential bleeding getting into the eyes and I didn't have to be told twice, I was so angry, and so my bandage was getting tighter and tighter with each wrap. At the end, I secured the bandage by tying the ends together in a tight knot. "If nobody helps me," I thought, "I have to learn to help myself."

As I finished the bandaging, I lifted my head up proudly to look at all those cowards in my class who didn't want to help. But in the very next instant I realized that I could not see. I could not see because I had bandaged not just my head but also my eyebrows and I did it so tightly that the skin on my eyelids was now bulging out of the bandage, making it impossible to open my eyes. My hooded eyelids did not help the matter. My bandage skills might have saved me from possibly bleeding to death but also made me unable to see. In my desperation I tried tilting my head back and looking through the little gap of light, but that made me unstable on my feet and I almost lost my balance, but then was able to steady myself by finding a wall to hold on to.

I tried to undo the bandage but the knot was done too tight. And as I stood there in front of the class unsure of what to do next, I heard someone saying: "She looks like a mummy. She is an Egyptian – not a German," and the whole class broke out laughing. I was laughing too and I could hear something like laughter – a muffled sound, but definitely laughter – coming from Sergey Sergeevich.

"We need some scissors," he said, still laughing, "and a volunteer."

Oksana eventually came and cut me free.

At the end of the class, Sergey Sergeevich stated that the quality of my bandage was excellent, and it was tight enough to stop any potential bleeding. It was done a bit low but the general principles were executed very well. Also given that I was doing it in hostile territory, I deserved a good mark for my bravery. "You are a good soldier, Lena Wolf," he said, and he gave me five points, which is the highest mark one could get.

And then he turned to address the class and said that they should be ashamed that a German girl was the best in their class, and who will defend our country from the fascists?

"She will," someone shouted. The bell rang. I was still standing there as everyone ran past me on their way to the freedom of a class break. Sergey Sergeevich did not look at me and I did not look at him. He was my hostile territory.

We're Terrorists

Polina Zherebtsova

Translated from the Russian
by Sara Jolly and Irina Steinberg

Any second now I'll snap shut the clasp on my handbag and then there'll be an explosion.

Whoever would have thought that a tiny "clot" of energy, powerful enough to blow human bodies to bits, could be inserted into the metal catch of a smart crocodile-skin handbag?

The security team searched me at the entrance and let me through. They didn't find anything. I am simply a journalist on my way to do an interview.

A tight ring of presidential guards surrounds the airport perimeter but I calmly smile up at the sun, confident in the knowledge that my brothers-in-arms are lying in the thick grass, waiting for the signal: they will attack as soon as the bomb goes off.

The task I have been assigned is to stealthily work my way as close as possible to the enemy.

Wearing a floaty, white dress, perfectly teamed with an elegant black jacket, I look as if I'm fresh off the catwalk in Milan. Before snapping shut the clasp I take in one last breath of warm air and take one last look at the blue hills. Farewell!

My friends have been tortured in interrogation camps. I must take revenge for that. An eye for an eye, blood for blood; so it was that Moses preached to us.

So it was that twelve Chechen heroes took revenge in the winter of 1995 by throwing themselves under some Russian tanks and blowing them up.

So it is that I too will take revenge.

"You know the protocol?" someone in a grey raincoat asks me. "You mustn't take a seat until you are invited to. Here He comes."

"Alright. Thank you," I say, despising myself a little.

When we speak in our mother tongue our voices have a different tone. When we speak Chechen it sounds hoarse, wild, it seeks affirmation in its own echo, it's like a bird call in the mountains; but these words I utter now in Russian are alien, dead.

We have enemies within. We must fight and die. Dudayev said, " A slave who doesn't try to free himself deserves to be enslaved a second time."

Now I just need to shout, "There is no God but Allah" but I don't have time.

A bullet scorches my chest. As I lose consciousness I activate the explosive device.

"I've achieved martyrdom!"

"You're such a liar!" shouted Islam, a boy I didn't like, as he clambered out from behind the dustbin, armed with a toy sub-machine gun. He was the chief of the President's guards and in the game he was called Ivan.

"I got suspicious and killed you before you could do anything. I'm old school KGB. You didn't have time to activate the detonator."

"But the bomb went off all the same and everyone around was killed. You can't talk, you're dead."

"You're dead too, Polina, you silly!" retorted Katya, a sniper. She was sitting on the roof of a shed covered with a large net that had been used to store potatoes and watermelons in the old days, before the war. The sun was glaring straight into her eyes, making her squint.

"No, Polina's right. We won!" wailed my friend Khava whose hands were tied She wriggled and writhed at the unfairness of it.

I rushed to untie her – although I was supposed to be in Paradise, being greeted by angels. "You're not allowed to do that!" Islam-Ivan howled and fired at us with his sub-machine gun. Rat-tat-tat-tat. So then the Chechen Mahomed crawled out of the grass and gave him a kick.

Probably on that sunny June day in 1996 we would have gone on squabbling until evening about who was right and who was wrong if it were not for Anya mother, auntie Zhenya. Nine year-old Anya was pretending to be an alien space ship, observing the actions of pitiful little human beings from high up in the sky And she didn't take sides.

Aunty Zhenya looked down from her balcony and saw the whole gang of us in a huddle by the garage arguing about who was a rebel and who was a Russian soldier, and about how to attain martyrdom; "Who wants jam sandwiches?" she shouted.

We instantly forgot about the game and ran up to the first floor. Lovely auntie Zhenya had gone through the supplies she kept in the cellar for a rainy day and had brought up a couple of large jars of jam – apricot and raspberry! We ate our fill, ladling the jam onto bread that had just come out of the oven.

Little did we know what lay ahead of us. We were naïve enough to believe that the war was over, that we could now turn it into a silly game, even though we could hear gunfire in the streets of our city.

"I've made a condensed milk sandwich! I scraped the last bit from the bottom of the tin," I boasted to Khava who was stuffing herself with apricot jam. "There's none left for the rest of you."

"You have all the luck because you're in Paradise," sneered Islam. "As we all know, you've become a martyr."

POETRY

Requiem

Anna Akhmatova

Translated from the Russian
by Stephen Capus

Unmoved by the glamour of alien skies,
By asylum in faraway cities, I
Chose to remain with my people: where
Catastrophe led them, I was there.

1961

In the terrible years of the Yezhov terror I spent seventeen months queuing outside the prisons of Leningrad. On one occasion someone "recognized" me. It was a woman who was standing near me in the queue, with lips of a bluish color, and who, of course, had never before heard my name. And now, waking from that state of numbness which was characteristic of us all, she quietly asked me (for everyone spoke in a whisper in those days):
"And can you write about this?"
And I replied:
"I can."
And then something like a smile flickered across what was once her face.

April 1, 1957
Leningrad

Dedication

Mountains are known to bend beneath such sorrow
And mighty rivers to cease to run;
But the prison doors will still stand firm tomorrow,
And behind them the cells will still resemble burrows,
And sadness will long for death to come.
For some cool breezes blow as day is dawning,
Others rejoice in sunsets – but here
Our days are all alike, monotonous, boring:
The hateful grating of keys in locks each morning
And the tramp of boots are all we can hear.
We arose at dawn, as if to pray together;
Through the ravaged city we made our way;
And the morning sun was low in the sky, the Neva
Was veiled in mist as, paler than ghosts, we gathered
And the sound of hope seemed so far away.
The sentence falls… She feels the tears searing
Her eyes, and now she's all alone;
And they'll cast her down, their fingers tearing
The life from her heart, coarse and uncaring;
But she'll stagger on down her lonely road …
We were thrown together in hell – and yet still I miss them,
Those random friends; and I wonder where they are:
What memories crowd the bright full moon, what visions
Haunt them now in their cold Siberian prison?
And I send this farewell greeting from afar.

March 1940

Introduction

This was a time when the corpses
All smiled, as though glad to have died,
When the city, reduced to an adjunct
Of its prisons, looked on from the side,
When driven half crazy by suffering,
The ranks of condemned shuffled by
And the trains on the point of departure
Whistled a song of goodbye.
The star of death glimmered wanly,
Far below an innocent land
Was trampled by blood-stained jackboots
And crushed beneath black prison vans.

1

They took you as day was dawning,
Like a mourner I followed behind,
In the hallway the children were bawling,
The icon light guttered and died.
I'll never forget: when you kissed me –
The chill of your lips; on your brow –
Cold sweat. Now like wives throughout history,
I'll stand by the Kremlin and howl.

Autumn 1935
Moscow

2

Quietly flows the quiet Don,
The yellow moon, strolling along,

Enters a house without a care
And chances upon a shadow there.

Not long ago that shadow was still
A woman – but now she's lonely and ill.

Her husband is dead, her son is in jail.
Remember her in your prayers without fail.

3

No, this isn't me, this is someone else who is suffering.
I wouldn't be able to do it – but let what's happened
Be veiled in black cloth, let the lamps be removed …
                              And then night.

4

If only you'd known, wicked woman
Who once cared for nothing but fun,
Who used to be Petersburg's favorite,
That the day will finally come
When, along with three hundred others,
Clutching your parcel, you'll go
To wait in line while your tears
Burn through the New Year's snow.
The poplar tree sways near the prison
In silence – but so many lives
Are ending inside for no reason …

5

At the feet of the cruel hangman,
Prostrating myself, I've groaned –
For seventeen months, my terror,
My son, I've called you back home.
Everything's muddled forever,
To me it's no longer clear
Who's a beast, who's a human being,
And whether the end is near.
And incense and blossoming flowers
And tracks on a road leading nowhere
Are all that remain … From the sky
A huge star looks into my eyes
And I finally understand
That destruction is close at hand.

1939

6

The weeks flutter by on light wings;
What's happened – I scarcely can say:
How the white summer nights looked in
Through the bars of the cell where you lay,
How still they look down on you there
With the pitiless eyes of a hawk
While the voices of strangers talk
Of death and the cross which you bear.

1939

7

The Sentence

And I felt the heavy verdict,
So long anticipated, fall
On my living breast. No matter,
I'll manage somehow. After all,

I've so many chores to attend to:
I must turn my heart into stone,
I must liquidate all my memories
And learn how to live alone.

And if not ... Through my window summer
Is celebrating somewhere out of sight.
I've foreseen it: this house, so empty,
On this day, so desolate and bright.

Summer 1939

8

To Death

You'll come one day for certain – then why not now?
Life is so hard; and while I wait, I've dimmed
The light and left the door ajar to allow
You in your simple splendor to enter in.
Assume for this purpose whichever guise you like:
Burst in like a shell with its load of death;
Sneak in like a skillful burglar as midnight strikes,
Or kill me like typhus, inhaled with a breath.
Or tell once more the well-known story we all
Have heard so often by now it's grown stale,
In which the men in military caps will call
And make the janitor's face turn pale.
To me it makes no difference. Quietly flows
The Yenisey. The North Star shines above.
All I can do is watch as terror enfolds
In mist those bright blue eyes I loved.

August 19, 1939
The Fountain House

9

I'm drunk on the harsh wine of madness
And all but concealed beneath
Its wing; and now it invites me
To enter the valley of death.

And I knew that I had to acknowledge
Defeat: that now it was time
To obey these delirious ravings
As if they weren't even mine.

And it won't allow me to carry
Any of my memories away,
However I try to persuade it,
Whatever I do or say:

Not the eyes of my son, filled with terror –
His suffering as adamant as fate,
Nor the day of the storm's arrival,
Nor the vigil at the prison gate,

Nor the hands' seductive coolness,
Nor the restless shadow of the lime,
Nor the sound of words offering comfort
From afar for one last time.

> *May 4, 1940*
> *The Fountain House*

10

Crucifixion

1

Don't weep for me, Mother,
As I lie in my grave.

Choirs of angels hymned the glorious hour,
Dissolved in flame, the heavens glowed overhead.
"Why hast thou forsaken me, my Father?"
And "Mother, do not weep for me," he said.

2

Magdalen sobbed and wrung her hands in anguish,
The disciple whom he loved was still as stone.
But no one dared to look toward the place where
The Mother stood in silence, all alone.

1940-43

Epilogue 1

I learned how to read the meaning of downcast faces,
To notice the way in which terror furtively peeks
From beneath half-lowered lids, how suffering traces
Its stern cuneiform script on ravaged cheeks,
How the hair which only the day before appeared
Lustrously black, can turn ashen gray overnight,
How smiles can fade on trembling lips and jeers,
However dry, can betray a tremor of fright.
And if I now venture to offer up this prayer,
It's not for myself alone, but rather for all
Who, enduring the changing weather, stood with me there
Beneath the indifferent gaze of that blank red wall.

Epilogue 2

Once more the hour of remembrance draws near
And it's almost as though I can see them all here:

The one who queued to the point of collapse,
And the one whose time on this earth has now passed,

And the one, who shaking her head, used to groan:
'When I enter this place, it's like coming back home!'

And I would have recorded you all in my verse,
But they've taken the list where your names were preserved.

So instead I've made you a shawl out of words,
Saved from the talk which I once overheard.

And I'll never forget you, wherever I go,
Whatever new horrors I'm destined to know.

And even if one day they somehow suppress
My voice through which millions of lives were expressed,

I ask that you all still remember to pray
For my soul on the eve of my burial day.

And if in the future they give the command
To raise up a statue to me in this land,

I consent to this honor – but only so long
As they solemnly pledge not to place it upon

The shore of the sea by which I was born,
For my link with the sea has long since been torn;

Nor in the park of the Tsars, by the tree
Where a restless soul is still searching for me;

But to raise it instead near the prison's locked door
Where I waited for three hundred hours and more.

For I fear I'll forget in the vacuous peace
Of the grave that old woman who howled like a beast,

Or the rumbling wheels of the black prison vans,
Or the sound of the hateful jail door when it slammed.

And from motionless eyelids the melting snow,
Like tears, down my cheeks of bronze will flow

As the dove in the watchtower calls from on high
And the boats on the Neva go drifting on by.

March 1940
The Fountain House

Four Poems

Svetlana Evdokimova

Translated from the Russian
by Stephen Capus

The Rooks Will Return

Churches and Easter cakes,
Samovars, bread freshly baked,
Don't loiter, keep up, move on,
The Muscovites hurry along.

The Muscovites' hands are so cleanly,
From the monastery through to the Kremlin,
The Lubyanka's cells are so pure,
Not empty, but clean, to be sure,
On his pension, the hangman's secure,
With clean hands he bakes bread, warm and fresh,
His hard work been crowned with success.

Beauty is all around,
And cleanliness also is found
In Moscow, but beauty's not cheap
And the price of clean hands can be steep,
Marmeladova's rouge cost a lot
And meanwhile the price hasn't dropped.

On Tverskaya Muscovites rush,
On the pavement a girl holds a sign:
"Be quiet, everyone, hush!"
You, too, be more reticent, please;
Both Tyutchev and Galich with time
Modestly held their peace.

The Muscovites hurry along,
Stay silent and bake your cakes,
The rooks will return before long,
Till then, be quiet and wait!

In the Museum of the Leningrad Blockade

In the Blockade Museum visitors can read
The words of a girl whose loved ones all died,
One after another. Then she died, too,
Died in a refuge for children.
She couldn't survive.

When all these things happened you still weren't born,
Nor had your mother yet met your father.
But something arose from the girl
Who couldn't survive the blockade,
Something began in that moment
When a weight fell on the city,
On the city as though on a scale,
Pressing it down to the earth,
The city which resembled a chalice,
The chalice she couldn't decline,
That chalice of mines
Which was drained to the lees by the people who still can be seen
On the walls of the Blockade Museum.

In that moment something was born
Through the immaculate conception of the word,
Something that's displayed there, still,
On the walls of the museum and which, now,
Like a seed, is received by my thoughts.

And I'll bear your words, little girl,
I'll bear them in the womb of my mind
And in it will blossom
Gratitude.

Requiem

Today I buried a bird.
She didn't fly, she came to me on foot
And settled by the wall near the house,
Beside a pipe from which water dripped
Onto the stone which seemed to serve her as a plinth.
There she stood, motionless,
Like a statue of bronze, while the busy flies,
Trying to outstrip time, alighted on her head
And even on her eyes, on her living eyes,
And on her beak, which was closed.
Are you dying, bird, or reflecting
In feathered despair on life and that final flight
To which your wings can no longer raise you up?
What questions, bird, are you struggling to answer
As you gaze on eternity, oblivious now
To the sky, to the trees – seeing only the wall
And the stone by the bush which for you has become
A tombstone, as well as a plinth?
Wearily, indifferently, the bird
Shakes an importunate fly from her beak and then blinks,
All alone with her mortal sadness.
Vainly life hurries by – the flights and the songs,
The worms, the midges, and even the seeds.
Do you remember, bird, the nests you built,
The food you bore in your beak
To your ungrateful, yellow-mouthed brood?
Do you remember the carefree carols
And the bliss of the morning sun?
Bird, you're dying, bidding farewell to the world,
Amazed that it's over so soon.
Vainly life hurries by, all the troubles,
The fledglings, the mislaid feathers and even
The fly that crawls on your beak.

What can I do? The water drips
And you're dying, bird, the way droplets die
As slowly they trickle, never to return,
From the pipe to the earth below.

Bird, oh, my bird,
You once used to fly …

* * *

My friend, here's my hand, here's my cheek,
I'm the brother, the sister you seek,
Here's my essence – my nature, the one
Human substance from which we all come,
Because you are the flesh of my flesh,
Just as I am of yours, no less.

My friend, don't shun me, I say,
My friend, don't chase me away,
Together let's live out our days
In our corners – me here and you there,
And between us one line – which we share.

Glass Balloon: A Triptych

Anna J. Jasinska

Introduction

This series of poems is inspired by the lives of young Polish people in Nazi-occupied Warsaw during the Second World War. The triptych is based on actual events from the beginning of August 1944, the first days of the Warsaw Uprising. The protagonist is a Polish teenager, Maria Radomska. Nearly seventeen years old when the Uprising broke out on August 1, 1944, she was my grandaunt and told me her story. Born August 19, 1927, Radomska, like many young people of her generation, was involved in the Polish Resistance Movement against the Nazi occupation. She was a Girl Scout in Gray Ranks (Szare Szeregi) from 1941, and then joined the Home Army (Armia Krajowa) in 1944. She served as a stretcher-bearer during the Warsaw Uprising. Following the Uprising, she became a prisoner of war. Together with other female Polish soldiers, she was transported from Warsaw to Altengrabow and then Oberlangen in Germany, where she was imprisoned in Stalags XI A and VI C, respectively. After Stalag VI C in Oberlangen was liberated on April 12, 1945, by the Polish 1st Armored Division, she joined the Polish II Corps in Italy. Later, she became a professor of agrotechnology and taught in the Wrocław University of Environmental and Life Sciences and the University of Rzeszów in Poland. She died April 8, 2018.

Ether (1)

It is my first job.
So first, so big – I can't breathe.
It was all my idea.

I volunteered to go
into town, not far,
two districts over,
across the battles in the streets.
My aunts don't expect me,
but they expect that someone
will come. Always.
They have guests at home –
two women from the Ghetto,
smuggled out
at night. Two years ago.

They're overjoyed to see
I am alive. I have a job.
Though I'm too young
to join the Home Army,
and we don't have a home.
It is a paradox called war.

Thankfully,
a bulbous bottle is there,
as usual, as I had hoped –
a wine-making demijohn,
dark. We call it a balloon,
but it is an apothecary flask
of flint glass, leak-tight,
with a ground stopper.
The bottle contains an iron wire
and five liters of liquid –
ether.

A sweet and sharp aroma.
Impossible, I can't smell it.
The bottle is sealed. Ether
sways on the walls, not much.
I am careful, on tiptoes.
It won't explode – the iron wand
is inside, like a lightning rod,
protecting it from a blast.

I fly on my feet.
The streets are blocked. Barricades rise up.
I stop in a gateway, catch my breath,
and tighten my hug of the glass balloon.
Soon, I hear *tap-tap*.
My weasel footsteps don't clang.
Tap-tap comes from behind,
then stops.
I think I should stop too –

close by, a high school.
I almost miss a hand-painted board:
Beware! Gunfire!
I know this school –
it's like the others – classrooms and corridors,
and, now, machine gun nests.
They overlook the street.
It's wide. No cover,
but a way across via a freshly dug trench.
They will spot me soon.
I must cross – I hug the glass balloon.

In the ward, they wait.
Bullets and shrapnel, sometimes
limbs set to be removed,
chips of the cracked bones too,

except for those better left inside,
in the skull
or close to an artery.

The doctors don't work long.
The anesthesia wears off.
A clock is blind and deaf.
Not I.

Crossing (2)

I step
into a narrow ditch.
I step
over those who had been crossing previously.

Except,
I have had luck, so far.
Except,
ether is volatile.

Because it is my job –
the glass balloon can't escape.
Because it is my job –
I am responsible, nobody else.

Except,
I could be swept by gunfire
or fall.
Except,
ether burns
like hell.

Warm (3)

I am an orderly,
seventeen in two weeks.
and helpless,
like a thermometer.
A stretcher-bearer.
A Girl Scout in a four-girl crew.
We check the vital signs
and bring the wounded from the streets.

Some survive.
Some, I push into a ditch –
the bodies feel cold.
One is warm. I report immediately.
Temperature is not evidence of life.
They confirm –
dead, for sure, dead.
I'm not convinced
not even now,
not even when I dream about him at night.

The Crimean Sonnets

Adam Mickiewicz

Translated from the Polish
by Kevin Kearney

To the companions of my Crimean voyage
– Adam Mickiewicz, 1826

Who would a poet understand
Must travel to the poet's land.
– Goethe in "Chuld Nameh," *West-Eastern Divan*

The Akerman[1] Steppe

I plunge into a dry and boundless sea of green:
Tall grass breaks round this wagon as around a boat;
Through waves of rustling meadows, through the flowers afloat,
I steer past thistle reefs and thorn isles in between.

The dark descends: no road nor barrow can be seen.
I scan the sky for stars to guide through this remote
Terrain. Has dawn arrived? Are distant clouds alight?
The Dniester shines in glow from Akerman's demesne!

Let's stop! How still! I hear the crane flock overhead,
So high that falcon eyes cannot discern their place.
I hear the bending wings of butterflies below,

Near grass where serpents slither through their meadow bed.
My ear craves to hear strains amid this silent space
From Lithuania, home. But no one calls, let's go!

This steppe is located northwest of Odessa near the city of Akerman (today Bilhorod-
Dnistrovskyi). It's from here that Mickiewicz began his journey through Crimea. The ancient fort of Akerman, with its lighthouse, dates from the thirteenth-fourteenth centuries.

Calm Sea
Upon the Heights of Tarkhankut[2]

A gentle wind caresses harbor flags in rows;
A swell from the sea's tranquil bosom seems to rise,
As if a bride dreamt blissfully with languid eyes,
And then awakened, sighed, and sank back to repose.

The sails hang silently like flags from battles past
On naked spars; the sturdy vessel softly rocks
As if enchained. One sailor sighs upon the docks,
While travelers now erupt in laughter round the mast.

O sea! There dwells amid your rich redoubt of life
A polyp sleeping in the depths when storm clouds brood,
But in the calm, it lashes forth tentacular taws.

O thoughts! A hydra-head of memories is rife
With pain: it rests and sleeps when passions rule your mood;
But into a calm heart it sinks its razor claws.

---

2   Tarkhankut is the westernmost cape of Crimea.

Sailing

The howling sea! The haunting phantom waves arise.
A sailor climbs the ladder: Children, be prepared!
He climbs the ladder further and, web-mesh ensnared,
Hangs like a lurking spider far above all eyes.

Wind! Wind! The vessel lurches as thick sea-foam flies:
It gnaws the bit, breaks free, and gallops unimpaired
Forward through froth-storms; clouds streak by, are sheared
To tatters as gusts fill the sails against blue skies.

My thoughts sway in the heavens like the rocking mast
Above; imagination, like these sails in course,
Sparks a spontaneous cry that joins the cheerful crew;

I drop upon my knees onto the deck, arms cast
Apart. My heart, it seems, is more a driving force
Than wind. Such lift and lightness now, as if I flew.

The Storm

Sails torn, the rudder broken, noise of waves, the roar,
Voices of anxious sailors, pumps in grating wail;
Ripped from the crewmen's hands, the straining lanyards fail,
While sun sinks into gloom, and hope dies at its core.

In triumph, the wind whines; and far from rocky shore,
Out of the wave-high sea, death rises midst the gale
And steps aboard the ship astride the mast and sail,
Much like a soldier breaching walls that hold no more.

One lies near-dead on deck; and there one wrings his hands;
And in the arms of friends, another says good-bye;
And others pray that they be spared the scythe of death.

But only one, alone among the party, stands
And thinks how blessed are those who, in a prayer, may die,
Or who have someone near to hear their final breath.

A View of the Mountains from the Kozlov[3] Steppe

The Pilgrim

Up there! Did Allah fashion this ice-sea expanse?
Was this throne carved for angels out of frozen falls?
And from one fourth the globe, did Devs[4] erect these walls
To stop the march of stars from eastern provenance?

It glows![5] Is Istanbul aflame in radiance
Above? Or did Allah, once night spread dun-gray palls
Like hilats[6] cross the sky, ignite the starry halls
Of heaven to alight the world in luminance?

Mirza[7]

There? I have been up there, where winter reigns: the beaks
Of brooks and throats of streams drank from its nest of ice,
And where I walked, my breath fell to the ground as snow.

No eagle ventured to these heights: I gazed from peaks
At clouds below, where thunder rolled down precipice
Of night, and overhead a single star did glow.
That's Chatyr-Dag[8]!

---

3   Kozlov is a small harbor on the west coast of Crimea. The region between Kozlov and the western foothills of Crimea is called the Kozlov Steppe.

4   Devs: according to ancient Persian mythology, these are malicious genii who once ruled the earth, then were banished by angels and now live at the end of the world, beyond Mount Kaf. [Author's footnote.]

5   At sunset, the summit of Chatyr-Dag seems to be on fire for some time owing to the reflection of the sun's rays. [Author's footnote.]

6   Hilat: an honorary dress that the sultan bestows on great state officials. [Author's footnote.]

7   Mirza: a Persian title of honor and distinction that is added to the name of the individual granted the title.

8   Chatyr-Dag: according to Mickiewicz, it is "the highest mountain on the south coast of Crimea and can be seen from up to 200 versts [around 220 kilometers] from all

The Pilgrim

Ah![9]

---

directions as a large bluish cloud." There are larger mountains in the Crimean range, but Chatyr-Dag is certainly the most imposing due to its position.

9 The exclamation "Ah!" expresses the pilgrim's surprise about the Mirza's courage and about the wonders he witnessed at the summit of the mountain. [Author's footnote.]

Bakhchysarai[10]

Still grand, this palace of Giray stands desolate.
Where once the brows of pashas burnished these stone halls,
Filled with divans, proud thrones, and coves of love, there crawls
A brood of reptiles now, and locusts congregate.

Through colored windows, bindweed creepers penetrate
And coil into the ceiling vaults and clutch the walls;
And nature thus reclaims the works of men: it scrawls
"RUIN," like ghost-hand meting out Belshazzar's[11] fate.

A vessel carved from marble still adorns the court[12],
A harem fountain which, despite the waste around,
Continues to drip pearly tears and to exclaim:

"Where have you fled, love, power, earthly fame?
You should endure forever; but soft water sound
Is all that still remains – O shame! – Your time was short."

---

10   In the valley, surrounded by mountains on all sides, lies the city of Bakhchysarai,
once the capital of the Girays, the Crimean khans. [Author's footnote.] Bakhchysarai
means "The Palace of Gardens."

11   "Suddenly the fingers of a human hand appeared and wrote on the plaster of the
wall, near the lampstand in the royal palace. The king watched the hand as it wrote."
Prophecy of Daniel 5:5 and 5:25-28. [Author's footnote.] This is in reference to the passage
in the Old Testament (Daniel 5:5) that describes King Belshazzar at a sumptuous banquet
during which a ghost-hand prophesies his downfall with enigmatic charactery on the wall
(mene, mene, tekel, parsin).

12   On the ground floor of the main body of the palace, in the hall of the courtroom,
there is the famous Selsebil, or Fountain of Tears.

Bakhchysarai at Night

The pious faithful leave the mosques in silent flows,
The muezzin's voice dissipates into the night.
Abashed, the dusk glows ruby-red; in silver light,
The moon entreats his mistress to a soft repose.

In heaven's harem, stars arrayed in shining rows
Illuminate in sapphire space a cloud in flight,
Which, like a sleepy swan with breast of gold and white,
Floats on a lake of black and, in the moonlight, glows.

The shadows fall from cypress crowns and minarets,
While granite giants tower in ebon arc around,
Arrayed on Iblis'[13] black divan like Satan's seed

Under the tent of darkness. Sometimes, without sound,
Lightning bolts, like white arrows launched from craggy heights,
Pierce the blue desert, swift as Fāris[14] on his steed.

---

13   Iblis, or Eblis, or Garazel refers to Lucifer in the Muslim faithful. [Author's footnote.]

14   Fāris: a knight among the Bedouin Arabs. [Author's footnote.] His horse is purported to have supernatural speed.

The Grave of a Potocka[15]

Amidst delightful orchards in the land of spring,
You withered, young rose! For the moments of your past
Flew forth like golden butterflies and could not last,
Giving way to the canker of remembering.

Toward Poland to the north, stars shine in brilliant ring,
Why do so many line this path? Are they the cast
Of your gaze full of fire before its brightness passed
Into the grave, in flight forever on the wing?

O Polish flower! In lonely mourning, my days shall
Expire, as well: may friends drop earth upon my tomb!
Travelers often gather here to honor you,

And their familiar accents will be like a call
Awaking me; for poets singing in this gloom
For you will see my grave nearby and touch me, too.

---

15   The Grave of a Potocka: Near the Palace of the Khans, there is a grave that has a
round dome and is built in an oriental style. There is a legend among the populace in
Crimea that this monument was erected by Khan Kerim Giray for a slave with whom he
shared an extraordinary love. The slave is purported to be a Polish woman, born a Potocki.
However, Muraviev-Apostle, the author of the beautiful and well-written work called
Travels in Crimea, maintains that the legend is without basis in fact and that the tomb actually contains the body of a Georgian woman. We don't know what he bases his opinion
on, since his assertion that the Tatars in the middle of the eighteenth century could not so
easily have kidnapped female slaves from the Potocki house seems unfounded. It is common knowledge that the most recent Cossack disturbances reported in Ukraine resulted
in many people being kidnapped and sold to the neighboring Tatars. There are numerous
noble families named Potocki in Poland, and the aforementioned captive might not have
necessarily belonged to the wealthy house of the heirs of Uman, which was less accessible
to the Tatar invasions or to the Cossack raids. The local legend of the Bakhchysarai tomb
was used by the Russian poet Alexander Pushkin as the basis of his poem *The Fountain of
Bakhchysarai*. [Author's footnote.]

The Harem Graves[16]

Mirza to the Pilgrim

The unripe grapes plucked from love's vineyard now lie here,
Once served at Allah's table: these pearls of the east,
Snatched from the sea of youth and happiness, deceased
Before their time, rest in this conch-like sepulcher.

The dark veils of oblivion and time obscure
Their grave, above which a cold turban[17], coiled and creased,
Shines like a tug[18] to troops of shadows; but at least
A heathen[19] hand has etched the names of those who were.

O Eden's roses! In your virgin purity,
Your days fell like chaste blossoms under modest pall
Of leaves, forever hid from gaze of infidel.

Now foreign eyes besmirch your grave – because of me!
Have mercy on my soul, great Prophet! But note well:
This foreigner alone sheds tears to honor all.

---

16   In a delightful garden, among the slender poplars and mulberry trees, there stand the white marble tombs of the Khans and Sultans, their wives and relatives; in two neighboring sites there are orderless tombs that were once well-maintained, but today are only decorated with bare boards and funereal drapes. [Author's footnote.]

17   Cold turban: Muslims will build stone turbans over the graves of men and women, with a different shape depending upon the gender of the deceased. [Author's footnote.]

18   Tug: a pole with horse or yak tail hairs of varying colors circularly arranged at the top. It was used during the period of the Mongol Empire and later adopted in derived Mongol and Turkic khanates. In the seventeenth century, it was taken up by Slavic Cossacks and Haidamaks under the name *bunchuk* (Ukrainian) or *buńczuk* (Polish), and it is still in use in the Polish military.

19   Heathen: Giaour means "unfaithful." This is what Muslims call Christians. [Author's footnote.]

Baidary[20]

I give my horse free rein and do not spare the lash;
In swift succession, valleys, boulders, woods pass by
Beneath my feet; like waves upon a stream, they fly;
And I imbibe these images in drunken dash.

But when my foam-mouthed horse obeys no more, and sash
Of evening's veil is loosed and colors leave the sky,
Then like fragmented mirrors on my burning eye
These images of valleys, boulders, forests flash.

Earth is asleep; not I. Into the sea, I run;
A black and foam-topped wave comes rushing up the shore;
I drop my head and stretch my arms toward the roar

Of water crashing in chaotic swirl. All thought
Is turning in this whirlpool, like a vessel caught;
And for a while my mind drowns in oblivion.

---

20   Baidary: a beautiful valley on the way to the southern shore of Crimea. [Author's footnote.]

Alushta[21] *by Day*

The mists, like hilat robes, slip down the mountainside,
The wheat fields, golden-coiffed, hum with the morning prayer.
The forest bows, spills rosaries[22] from its vernal hair
With rubies, garnets, gems to suit a khalif's pride.

The meadows are in flower, and blossoms sail cross wide
Expanse, with rainbow butterflies; and in the air,
A baldachin[23] of diamonds veils the sky. Elsewhere,
In wing-shaped shrouds, the whirring locust swarms abide.

And where bald-pated cliffs look in a watery glass,
Waves rise and seem to gather for a new attack,
While, in their surge, light plays as if in tigers' eyes,

Foretelling that a greater storm will come to pass;
But there, where deepest waters shimmer blue and black,
The flocks of swans and vessels float beneath calm skies.

---

21   Alushta: one of the most delightful places in Crimea: here, there are never northerly
winds; and even in November, the traveler often finds relief from the heat under the shade
of huge walnut trees that are still in leaf. [Author's footnote.]

22   Muslims use rosaries during their prayers, which in the case of distinguished people
are sometimes studded with expensive stones. Pomegranate and mulberry trees, redden-
ing with delightful fruit, are common throughout the entire southern coast of Crimea.
[Author's footnote.]

23   Baldachin: a golden silk curtain over a chair or a cover on poles draped over a high-
ranking person, used during processions and ceremonial celebrations.

Alushta at Night

The breeze feels brisk; the arid winds of day abate.
The back of Chatyr-Dag glows in the parting beams,
Which spill and crash in crimson like celestial streams,
Then fade. The pilgrim listens in a watchful state:

The valley now is mute, the mountain black as slate;
On cornflower bed, the springs are murmuring in their dreams;
The vibrant air, suffused with floral perfume, seems
Only to reach the heart: the ear is insensate.

I fall asleep beneath the quiet wings of night,
Then am awakened by a blazing meteor
That lights up mountain, vale, and sky in golden shine.

O eastern night! Like odalisque[24] of orient, your
Caresses soothe to slumber; yet, dare I recline
To sleep, you rouse again with sparkling eyes alight.

---

4   Odalisque: a word of Turkish origin (*odalık*), referring to a woman who serves the
ladies of the Sultan's harem; generally, a flirtatious, passionate woman.

Chatyr-Dag

Mirza

Trembling, the Muslim kisses your rock feet. O mast
Of the Crimean ship, great Chatyr-Dag! You rise,
Minaret of the world, and tower into the skies,
The padishah[25] of mountains in eternal cast!

You sit in majesty at heaven's portal, vast
And tall, like Gabriel[26] guarding Eden's edifice;
The forest is your cloak, and lightning bolts incise
Your cloudy turban as if janissaries[27] passed.

And whether sun oppresses or the fog is cold,
Or locusts strip our fields, or giaours burn houses down,
O Chatyr-Dag, you are impassive, still, and terse!

You straddle earth and sky, the dragoman[28] of old,
With people, lands, and thunderbolts beneath your crown,
And you but hear what God says to the universe.

---

25   Padishah: the title of the Turkish Sultan. [Author's footnote.]

26   Gabriel: I use the name Gabriel here because it is well known. In eastern mythology, the guard of the heavens is actually Ramek, one of the two large stars called "*As semekein.*" [Author's footnote.]

27   Janissaries: dangerous Turkish infantry.

28   Dragoman: Arabic for interpreter or translator.

The Pilgrim

This land of beauty and abundance has no peer:
Blue sky above, and lovely faces greet my gaze.
Why does my heart go truant, dwell upon a phase
Of life far off in time and place, yet still so dear?

The Baidar nightingales and virgins of Salgir[29]
Sing less sweet than your forests, Homeland! Your damp ways
Through somber bogs delight me more than golden glaze
Of pineapples and red mulberries growing here.

So distant! And such different lures command my mood.
Why am I so distracted, sighing endlessly
For her, whom I loved in the morning of my years?

And in the cherished home I lost, she now appears,
Where once, as faithful lover, I devoutly stood.
She treads on my fresh tracks: does she remember me?

---

29 Virgins of Salgir: Salgir, a river in Crimea, flowing from the caves of Chatyr-Dag.
Author's footnote.] The Salgir river is the longest river on the Crimean Peninsula.

Path at the Precipice of Chufut-Kale[30]

Mirza

Say a prayer, free the rein, avert your eyes from this.
The rider trusts his horse's footing here[31]: the steed
Is brave, exact, and grabs the cliff's edge with strong-kneed
And supple legs, while eyeing depths in the abyss

Suspended! Here, do not look down: your eyes will miss
Their target, as in well of Al-Khaír. No need
To point your wingless arm at anything; instead,
Abandon thinking, for all thought is precipice

Of ruin, anchor pulling down in chaos, where
It hits like bolt of lightning; and your vessel then
Will not find ground, but drift in darkness without aim.

Pilgrim

Mirza! I did look down through earth's rifts gaping there!
And what I saw, I will recount, but only when
Interred: these sights were more than mortal words can frame.

---

30 Chufut-Kale: a town on a lofty rock; the houses standing on the edge of the precipice resemble swallow's nests. The path leading up is severe and exposed to the abyss. In the city itself, the walls of the houses are almost flush with the edge of the chasm. When you look out the window, your gaze is lost in an immeasurable depth. [Author's footnote.]

31 The Crimean horse seems to have a special instinct for caution and safety in difficult and dangerous passages: before it takes a step, it holds its foot in the air and looks for a secure stone, then tests whether it is safe or not. [Author's footnote.]

Mount Kikineís[32]

Mirza

Look down in the abyss: those heavens lying there
Are the sea. From its waves, a bird-mount[33] seems to rise,
Lightning-impaled, with mast-like feathers that comprise
A semicircle wider than a rainbow where

An isle of snow masks watery fields as blue as air.
That island sailing in the depths is cloud[34] the size
Of Simurgh: she cloaks half the world in gloomy guise
Of darkness. Can you see her fiery-ribboned hair?

Lightning has struck! Let's wait. The chasm at the base
Must be spanned at full gallop; I will leap this gap,
And you remain behind with ready spur and whip.

When I have ridden, look across at that cliff face:
If you see feather shining, it is in my cap.
If nothing, then no man should ever dare this trip.

---

32   Kikineís is a Tatar settlement between the Baidar Pass and the southern coast of
Crimea.

33   The bird-mount is known from *One Thousand and One Nights*. It is famous in Persian mythology and known as the bird Simurgh, described many times by Eastern poets.
According to Ferdowsi in *Shahnameh*, it is "as great as a mountain, and strong as a fortress
and can lift an elephant in its talons," and further: "Seeing the knights, Simurgh sprang
up like a cloud from the rock on which he lives and flew through the air like a hurricane,
casting a shadow over the horsemen's army." [Author's footnote.]

34   "This island sailing in the depths is a cloud!": From the top of the mountains, which
rise above the clouds, we can look down at the clouds flowing over the sea; and it seems as
if they lie directly on the water in the shape of large white islands. I observed this interesting phenomenon from Chatyr-Dag. [Author's footnote.]

The Castle Ruins of Balaklava[35]

These castles, now just heaps of rubble, proudly stood
In your defense, Crimea, ever thankless land.
Like giant skulls, their hulls jut upward: once so grand,
They now house reptiles and men baser than this brood.

I climb the turret, seeking bygone signs that would
Reveal chivalric past, the marks of one who manned
These stations: hero, soldier, now engulfed in sand
Of time's oblivion, like worm wrapped in grape-leaf shroud.

Here, a Greek once inscribed Athenian ornaments,
And there, Italian warriors felled the Mongol scourge
With iron, here a Meccan pilgrim said his prayer.

Today, black wings of vultures circle in the air,
As if in city ravaged by a pestilence,
Where flags in mourning wave to rhythms of a dirge.

---

35   Above the bay of this same name, there stand the ruins of a castle that had been buil
long ago by Greeks arriving from Miletus. Later, the Genoese built the fortress of Cemba
on this site. [Author's footnote.]

Ayu-Dag[36]

Resting on cliffs of Ayu-Dag, I like to gaze
At foaming breakers in the surf: these waves in black
Battalions burst like snow upon the jagged stack
Of rocks, with myriad rainbows wheeling in the haze.

The waves make turgid motion, crashing in the bays
Like troops of whales along the shore in crazed attack
To claim the land in triumph, then receding back,
With mussels, pearls, and corals glittering in sun's rays.

And this is what it looks like, poet, in your heart:
Your passions brew foul weather, yet you grab your lyre
And find no inner turbulence can harm you now,

As pain sinks to oblivion, and eternal art
Of songs in verse emerge as crown from tempering fire,
With which the future ages will adorn your brow.

---

36   Ayu-Dag: between Yalta and Alushta on the southern coast of Crimea, this
promontory rises 572 meters above sea-level. It literally means "Bear Mountain": (*Ayu* –
bear; *Dag* – mountain).

Acknowledgements

This translation was inspired by Katharina Mommsen, Professor Emerita of German Literature at Stanford University, who gave a trilingual edition of *The Crimean Sonnets* (Polish, French, and German) to all attendees at her eightieth birthday celebration in 2005. Her enthusiastic response to the first draft of these English translations provided important motivation to continue working on and improving them.

Equally important in this process were the insightful comments of Boris Dralyuk, Editor-in-Chief of *Cardinal Points*, whose criticism was invaluable in providing guidance on what to prioritize in the translations and in working out the kinks of the first draft. Without his cooperative approach, quick response, and keen critical eye, these translations might have died on the hard drive of my laptop.

The website wolnelektury.pl (https://wolnelektury.pl/katalog/lektura/sonety-krymskie-motto-i-dedykacja.html) proved vital in providing not only the original poems in electronic form, but also very important footnotes, both those of the author and those of the website's editors, which offered historical and contextual information crucial to a full understanding of the original poems.

Finally, the English prose translations, notes, and interpretations of Charles S Kraszewski in Mickiewicz's *The Sonnets, Including the Erotic Sonnets, the Crimean Sonnets and Uncollected Sonnets* (Glagoslav Publications, 2018) were very helpful in gaining a complete understanding of the literal meaning of each poem, word by word.

Original English Verse in the Onegin Stanza

Antony Wood

Introduction

A number of writers have produced novels written in Onegin stanzas, most notably, to a British and American public, John Fuller (*The Illusionists*, 1980), Vikram Seth (*The Golden Gate*, 1986), and Andy Croft (*The Ghost Writer*, 2007). "Lightness" is a term that has often been used to characterize Pushkin's verse, and this quality is amply present in these original English uses of the Onegin stanza.

As it is in my own translations of Pushkin as well as my attempts at original verse which I've got into the habit of writing when I feel like it – unsurprisingly with Pushkinian stylistic impregnation. An example, now dating back a decade, is offered here in print for the first time in excerpts as I look over writings and translations done over the same period as much of the work included in my new Pushkin selection from Penguin Classics.

Eugene Onegin got inside my inner ear soon after I'd learned the basics of Russian during national service at the Joint Services School for Linguists. I remember discussing it with a young Russian ballerina to whom I had been introduced to practice my spoken Russian. We were both fascinated by the ambiguities in Pushkin's ironic overtones. Not long after completion of my formal education I drafted a version of the first two chapters – which I have kept in a bottom drawer ever since, watching the appearance of at least eight other British and American translations. I set about translating other verse of Pushkin instead. In 2020 my selection of Pushkin's lyric and narrative verse, in translations stored up and periodically revised over the years, was published.

The opportunities for prosodic acrobatics with the Onegin stanza are irresistible to anyone poised for original composition. In their full-length verse novels the above-mentioned have dazzled with present-day style, idiom, and settings. Seth gets a single word over a whole line: "Irreconcilability." I too have joined the fun, but with a good deal less of modern usage and setting and attempting to catch something of other notes to be heard in Pushkin's use of the form – which has free-roving expressive range, *mot juste* linguistic precision, rich sonic sensitivities, subtle variety of tone, register and mood – above all, a natural-sounding, genial narrative voice that miraculously seems to be the reader's own. The stanza's warmly dignified tone and free-flowing structure seem to me a perfect vehicle for sympathetic treatment of the life of a known and familiar person.

So it was the Onegin stanza that I used for a narrative portrait, lightly ironic but in an admiring tone, of an uncle of mine up to his 100th birthday, and then, after he continued to conduct his life at the same pace as before, finished off as a complete life at his death two years later. My main source was a résumé Uncle Francis had written in middle age to tell his children about his rather dramatic earlier life, to which I added my own and others' memories of him over his later years. Though the result deals throughout in what has reached me as "fact," not in flights of imagination (however much it might sometimes seem otherwise), it reads like verse fiction; in the first of its thirty-nine stanzas I call it a "verse novella," though it's really a sketch for a verse novel; I refer to it as a "novella" simply to rhyme with "fellow." The personal affection felt in the act of composition seems to me Oneginesque in spirit, though of course this piece of *vers de société* cannot emulate Pushkin in anything other than the matter of prosody.

Not long after *Portrait* was completed I found myself using the Onegin stanza again in two stanzas written in memory of Stanley Mitchell, after whose death in 2011 I was to be asked to translate the narrative parts of *The Bronze Horseman* to follow Stanley's version of the "Prologue," which was as far as he had got in his commissioned translation of the poem for *The Penguin Book of Russian Poetry*, edited by Robert Chandler, Boris Dralyuk, and Irina Mashinski.

Portrait of an Englishman

A Brief Life of W.F.B. Nott (1908–2010)
(Excerpts)

I

First you must meet my hero's father,
One Lewis Herbert William Nott.
You'll say: Why start with him? – I'd rather
Tell my tale *my* way. Let the plot
Of this my, call it, verse novella
(But fact) about a doughty fellow
Start with this officer, retired,
Of ancient family, much admired
For services to King and Country,
His spouse's folk, too, much revered.
Strangely, churchwise, the pair adhered
To tenets Low, at home with sundry
Brethren and Quaker radicals
And suchlike Evangelicals.

II

Now Lewis Nott was majordomo
To a wealthy lady, a Miss Bell,
The sort to summer on Lake Como;
She lived extraordinarily well.
Her steward helped her run a mission
In Tooting (really). Ever efficient,
He told her first of his new boy;
Miss Bell was overcome with joy
And willed his son substantial money,
But ... best laid plans of mice and men ...
She was to take it back again:
Sadly, though some may find it funny,
One day this boy kicked Bell's cook's shin –
Not just put down to Original Sin.

III

Uncle – really my Cousin[1] – Francis
(William Francis Bell, sic,[2] Nott)
When older was to seize his chances.
At school he didn't learn a lot
But took to music. So to Turin
To get his pianistic ear in.
He met, footloose and fancy free,
The Contessina Carassì.
His studies suffered, so his daddy
Put him on the next train home.
Now where shall my young scapegrace roam?
Will he turn out to be a baddy?
(The Contessina, I must add,
Married a prince who turned out *bad*.)

He married a first cousin of my father.

Our hero's first-intended benefactor may have withdrawn her money, but her name was not to be removed from the baptismal register.

IV

They say the son is like the father.
Our hero's, in the army line
Just like his father and *his* father,
With Allenby in Palestine
Had come home with a Social Conscience,
Which verged on … Communism. Such nonsense
His son could scarcely tolerate
And studied law with Tom Outhwaite.
Our art'cl'd clerk, a little lonesome,
Ventured to a tennis club
And, asked to make the numbers up,
Was partnered with a Joan E. Tomson.
She was a player to admire;
The two got on like a house on fire.

V

And went on doing so. Letters followed.
The aspiring lawyer won his set
(In an ancient Morris Oxford – borrowed)
With the Oxford undergraduette,
Both of them skint. But when the visitor
Became a qualified solicitor,
The moment had arrived for rings.
The wedding was at Charlton Kings.
The couple settled in the country,
Which made them lackadaisical;
And so to London – Rosslyn Hill.
Our lawyer joins the Hampstead gentry …
A TA signals company
Supported by the STC.[3]

Signals Training Centre, run by the British Army before and during the Second World War, most actively in India.

VI

Life with just the seven-fifty
A partner's salary brings in
Is hard; the pair must needs be thrifty;
Michael is joined by Carolyn.
With unemployment at its zenith
A Tory candidate for Erith
Was needed: lucky Party got
The youthful W. F. B. Nott.
But Hitler stopped the next election,
So no more polls till 'forty-five;
Our candidate was still alive
But didn't stand: upon reflection
There's nothing here that's very strange;
The war produced a lot of change.

VII

Our lawyer rose to wartime Colonel,
And Joan became the editor
Of the US Army Medical Journal,
For which they duly cited her.
Her husband chose to serve in India
(He turned down Iceland – colder, windier).
Lieutenant Nott at first, OC
5th F. R. Signals Section, he
Was soon promoted Captain for his
Signals achievements in the North.
The Army further saw his worth
And gave him charge of native forces:
Muslims, Hindus and Maharats,
Punjabis, Dogras, Sikhs and Jats.

VIII

Our Captain, now Lieutenant-Colonel,
Is posted to the Burma Front –
For Signals, nowhere more infernal:
A single track bears all the brunt
Thousands of miles through mostly jungle.
Here is not a job to bungle:
The poles for telegraph and phone
Have to be metal, wood'll be prone
After white ants have hollowed through it,
Exposing all the copperwire –
Elephants' 'satiable desire.
Nevertheless, and few to know it,
Wingate without Nott's expertise
Wouldn't have made it through the trees.

IX

One feat especially triumphal
Stands out in Regimental lore.
The road from Silchar east to Imphal
(Proud capital of Manipore),
With obstacles at all its stages –
Four rivers and three mountain ranges –
Vertiginous and full of holes,
Had to be lined with telegraph poles.
Our man took one last drive along it
Before the Japanese advance,
And there was more than half a chance,
Were he unduly to prolong it,
All trace of him would soon be gone:
The Burma Railway he'd be on.

[*… Years of postwar life in England as a lawyer, in business, and as an inveterate traveler …*]

XXXVI

The venerable Eastergater[4]
Cannot go on for ever; he
Has renal failure some months later,
At home. The visiting GP
Alerts the ever-caring Pamela,
Who signals to his friends and family
To come and say goodbye to him.
There in the sunlounge, groomed and trim,
Today in salmon linen jacket,
His favorite bold contrasting shirt,
And also meriting a word,
A faultless tie and neat wool waistcoat –
There he sits to greet his guests,
Enjoying memories, many jests.

---

4   After Joan's death our hero, aged eighty-nine, had settled in the village of Eastergate, near Chichester, West Sussex.

XXXVII

But now his voice is just a murmur;
He finds it hard to move his hand.
The veteran, 101, of Burma
However, still retains command.
The girl who's come to do the mowing
Calls for her money as she's going:
The fingers searching in a purse,
With Pamela by, are his, not hers.
A fragrant face draws near his: 'Gorgeous!'
He breathes, and then we take our leave.
Days later, comes the time to grieve.
The doctor had it right. Last orders –
The wines to toast next birthday health
Now serve the social rites of death.

XXXVIII

A man of infinite resources
And who was equal to his luck,
Who could adapt to different courses,
Adventurous as Tom or Huck;
At home with matters firmly factual,
Who charmed an Oxford intellectual;
A man, as I have said, of parts,
Soldier, lawyer, lover of arts;
Right, politically, of Jinghis
(He claimed), for a society
Where no one lives off you and me;
A man magnificently English,
A man who never lost the plot –
Such was William Francis Nott.

FINIS

To Stanley[5]

Admired by Bayley and Isaiah,
At Oxford you inspired the left,
And bore your fellows ever higher
Upon the wings of each bold heft.
When down, you'd praise to all who'd listen
The Russian Marxist *Germanisten*:
Lifshits, Dymshits … all the -shits;
You'd do the intellectual splits
Between the diktats of the Party
And something far more flexible –
Could Trotskyism fill the bill?[6]
Deep in your soul, though, you were arty:
The spell of Russian literature
It was that grasped and held you sure.

We can't be certain of the stage in
Your course of life when first you knew
Your dearest friend, Eugene Onegin;
Birmingham, though, where first you drew
Conclusions on *EO*'s digressions
In learned print, with no concessions
To your renowned antagonist,
The prime Italian Pushkinist.[7]
At Essex, broad course innovator,

Contribution to a celebration of the life of Stanley Mitchell at Pushkin House in London, March 6, 2012.

For some time after the demise of the East German Communist Party with the end of the Soviet era Mitchell was at serious ideological loss.

Ettore lo Gatto (1890-1983). In an article on some essays on the digressions in *Eugene Onegin* (*Slavonic and East European Review* 44, no. 102 [April, 1966]) Mitchell presented his own more convincingly subtle and thoroughgoing view of their integration into the narrative.

You led a study of *EO*
And noted all that one could know;
Then made for pastures new. Years later
You replaced, on his pedestal,
Charles Johnston with *your* miracle.

THE ART OF
TRANSLATION

"Seeking Ghosts of Clinking Coins"
Shelters and Travels with Anna Alekseeva

James Manteith

When Piotr Tarasov asked whether *Apraksin Blues* editor-in-chief Tatyana Aprak-sina might look at poetry by his aunt, Tatyana didn't know what to expect. A soft-spoken, neatly dressed introvert whose face, framed by a wiry white mane, often wore an expression of enigmatic mild irony, Piotr regularly attended our St. Petersburg gatherings. His own writing drew on patriotic passions for imperial military history and Cyrillic orthography.

Piotr's aunt was no longer living. Piotr dreamed of doing more for her work and felt unsure where to start. "Some of her poems have even been published," he told Tatyana. "I like some of her writing, but I don't know whether it'll be to your taste. You know best."

A longtime *Apraksin Blues* collaborator, I witnessed their deliberations. The year 2019 was drawing to an end. A longtime Petersburg friend, a counterculture mainstay colloquially known by the allusive moniker "Rodion," reported grapevine rumors of some calamity lurking in the New Year's auspices. Yet at our December departure we trusted in the integrity of the city and our ties there.

In January, back at our other base at the edge of a California wilderness Tatyana received a freshly keyboarded assortment of poems. That same day ominous news broke of a quarantine lockdown in China.

Left unprefaced by mention of their author's identity, the poems bore date and often referenced themes relatable to known history, in parallel with private and interior occasions. A first poem cheerily saluted the arrival of a New Year in the era just before the First World War. The closing selections, ending in the year of the Great Victory, reflected a firsthand endurance of the Siege of Leningrad. A 1922 poem memorializing Nikolai Gumilyov was among the signs of interaction with literary figures of the era. Many of the poems, Tatyana felt, contained line worthy of standing beside the lasting verse of their time. The poetry represente a distinctive new perspective as well as a significant cultural and historical source. Replying to Piotr, Tatyana suggested that the author merited the attention of more specialized literary venues, in parallel with publication in modest, multidisciplinary *Apraksin Blues*. Would Piotr permit such inquiries? Could he provide at least minimal information about the poet?

The author turned out to have lived from 1899 to 1945, probably separating her from Piotr by a couple of generations. We still didn't know her name.

In the month's last days, we received two biographical sketches identifying the poet as Anna Alekseeva. The shorter text was chronologically complete. The more detailed account, Piotr's own, as yet trailed off in 1924, a little more than midway through the poet's brief life.

Born in St. Petersburg as Anna Ivanova, one in a ten-child family, to the second wife of an Alexandrinsky Theater make-up artist, the future writer had come of age amid the seismic shifts of the First World War and the February and October Revolutions. As a young woman, she had taught drawing and Russian. While beginning a job as a librarian, she had fallen for an older, married man of some cultural prominence. A daughter from that affair had died in infancy.

Meanwhile, the young poet had earned an arts diploma and begun studies at Petrograd's progressive Institute of the Living Word, founded two years before and employing a roster of luminaries. In addition to Vsevolod Meyerhold and Anatoly Lunacharsky, she studied under Gumilyov, attending his final poetry seminars before his arrest and execution. She stuck with the institute's courses until its 1924 closure by officialdom.

That same year, Anna married fellow poet Vladimir Alekseev, the son of the idealist philosopher Sergei Askoldov. Alekseev, an old friend and sometime co-author of Alexander Vvedensky, mingled with a broad range of aspiring and established writers. Alekseeva intersected with the literary circles characteristic of her husband and the cultured Alekseev-Askoldov household. Then membership in the short-lived "Brotherhood of Seraphim of Sarov" society for religious philosophy led to Askoldov's exile. Eventually losing the family home, the Alekseevs moved to a small windowless room in a communal apartment off the Fontanka embankment.

Hosting ongoing meetings, the diminutive new lodgings remained part of grassroots support networks for intellectuals, including former members of unsanctioned cultural groups like Vvedensky and Daniil Kharms's "OBERIU." Yet Alekseeva, teaching Russian and literature and working as a librarian at a local school, understandably felt ambivalent about her life and creative direction.

Then the Great Patriotic War came. Alekseeva lost her husband to siege-time starvation. The couple's son, Nikita, finally evacuated, was drafted and then killed in his first battle. Alekseeva wrote poetry throughout the war. Yet less than two months after the Allied victory in Europe, she passed away in her mid-forties, exhausted and not quite able to rise from the ashes.

Alekseeva's archives had passed into the care of her niece, Natalia Tarasova. In the century's last decade, Tarasova collaborated on the initial posthumous publications in newspapers and a volume, sponsored by a memorial organization, of blockade-centered selections from letters and poetry. The "Pushkin House" Russian Literary Institute had acquired the father-and-son archives of Askoldov and Alekseev. Some of Anna Alekseeva's writing and story figures in Caroline Walton's 2011 *The Besieged*. Yet only a fraction of Alekseeva's surviving creative work had ever come to light.

Olga Bogdanova's literary encyclopedia of twentieth century literary Petersburg contains an edited version of the more polished biography we'd seen – in its published form, attributed to N. Tarasova and P. Tarasov – as well as Tarasova's entry on Vladimir Alekseev. In addition to less-official connections, Alekseeva's poet husband had begun literary activities as a member of the Soviet Writers' Union, which in time opted to expel him concurrently with Kharms and Aleksey Skaldin, part of loosely overlapping circles. Thereafter, although Alekseev kept writing poetry in his final decade, he no longer published. As nonconformist writers, both he and his entirely unprinted wife wound up marginalized and neglected.

Exiled Askoldov's last years were as grim as his son's and daughter-in-law's. Finding himself in a zone of occupation, he spoke out against Marxism. Evacuated to Potsdam's "Russian village" by retreating German troops, he was found dead when the advancing Soviets came to arrest him.

Such melancholy details defied casual response. Tatyana reviewed the biographies no more than perfunctorily, then set them aside, leaving their pertinence for others to interpret. In her etiquette of dialog, she preferred to concentrate on poetic acquaintance.

In late February, Irina Mashinski of *Cardinal Points* let us know that her longtime collaborator Maria Bloshteyn was wrapping up work on an anthology of English-language translations of Russian poetry from the Second World War. Bloshteyn confirmed that enough time remained for the anthology to include Alekseeva.

Meanwhile, Piotr made a new discovery: among his family archives, evidently recently inherited and not yet fully examined, a trove of original manuscripts. Before, he had worked from a compact set of typescripts. Estimating the new stack might total 500 pages, he now admitted "slight horror" at Alekseeva's actual quantity of surviving texts. The papers included shorter lyric poems and longer works. Newly unearthed poems might alter future conceptions of the author. Ideally, everything would need review to decide how to surface the poems. He couldn't guess how long the deciphering and typing might take.

Tatyana offered to take on this work while reading and editing from the archive, if Piotr would send scans. He gratefully accepted; even his batches of scanning would take him many months. For her part, Tatyana welcomed the possibility of long-deferred proper outcomes. In early March, Alekseeva's handwriting began to arrive in California.

Two photographs of Alekseeva hung above Tatyana's work desk. In the first, Alekseeva is still round-cheeked and girlish. In the second, from 1940, the poet has gained her adult face and a seemingly characteristic gaze, with hints of the demeanor of her archive's heir. Tatyana found the resemblance delightful, and told Piotr so.

As the new circulation of texts gained momentum, a pandemic vocabulary acquired global ubiquity. Piotr might fall silent for weeks at a time. We feared the worst for him and the manuscripts. He always reappeared, though, navigating his own patterns of disruption. Separated by continents, the partnership continued, with Anna Alekseeva a shared presence across our sheltering.

The arc of Alekseeva's literary consciousness came into focus – from juvenilia in the '10s to a sudden flowering during her studies and maturation in the '20s and early '30s, followed by a plateau in the late '30s and her war-shadowed final half-decade. In her most fertile period, Alekseeva had connected with her muse. Comprehending the force of poetry, she had felt the thrill of belonging to literature, even if perpetually relegated to its fringes, and had sought to maintain high standards.

The later poems, the main ones thus far given posthumous publication, remained priceless despite falling short of the undiscovered poet's promise. Increasingly isolated and vexed, Alekseeva had tended to settle for sketches, diaristically denoting moods and impressions across tides of ordeals. Amid blockade hunger, she had palpably, openly struggled to remain capable of connected thought at all.

Yet all of Alekseeva's work had a unique temperament and nerve, even as she sought her own voice. Her poems' psychological veracity, too, had all the more impact on us in the throes of the pandemic – not truly comparable to the far more devastating siege and Second World War, yet experienced as a related pall across the sun. Alekseeva's archive, which Tatyana worked on nearly every day, helped to maintain perspective. Restoration of both the anguished and confident poems served to reinforce a desperately needed bedrock of stamina.

Although cogent in appraising her apparent stagnation, Alekseeva had believed herself capable of reemergence. Indeed, the war had galvanized other poets for new levels of artistry. Alekseeva, despite her heroism in remaining prolific, had not quite found her own new hold on life. She sometimes expresses relatively incongruous intimations of greatness in poems marred by comparatively weaker lines. Yet somehow her talent, even when obscured, had always remained legitimately alive inside her, right through her wistfully forward-looking final lines, in Walton's translation, "There is my old dance dress/To patch up and mend." With the poignant suggestion, in Alekseeva's best poems, of the poet she might and ought to have been, involvement with her literary legacy felt like not only justice for her but a balm for all of us.

The thirtieth issue of *Apraksin Blues*, published in May in anticipation of our magazine's twenty-fifth anniversary, featured nineteen of the previously unpublished poems. More of the poet's manuscripts kept arriving. In July, Bloshteyn's *Russia is Burning*, delayed by the pandemic, finally appeared. The anthology combines original commentary with that Walton translation and a new co-translation, with Boris Dralyuk, from the recently rediscovered poems; Bloshteyn's closing essay on wartime poetry calls Alekseeva's poems "extraordinary."

By the time we received *Russia is Burning*, much of California was in flames. We twice had to evacuate. Throughout this, Tatyana kept working on Alekseeva. Upon our return, the anthology, lying on one of our office desks, appeared talismanic, prophetic, its vintage poster cover's heroine, clad in a crimson frock and kerchief, seeming to issue a stern summons.

Suddenly, unconditionally, we felt that we needed to be back in St. Petersburg soon, at least within this crucial year. Before the pandemic had struck, we had planned to return there in the autumn. The situation remained daunting, but we decided to risk travel anyway. In November, we flew the sole air route to Russia that remained open for us. The gates of Istanbul, through which Gumilyov had passed, became our portal to Petersburg.

Russia is Burning, the first thing I'd packed, went directly into Piotr's hands when he came by our Petersburg office that winter. He sent more scans, which Tatyana now typed from at her Petersburg desk. Raisa Reznik's literary journal *Svyaz Vremyon (The Time Joint)* included eleven more of the unpublished poems in an issue released on New Year's Eve.

Alekseeva's work continued to color my perceptions. Her own era was substantially more recent than the classical and *art nouveau* architecture of the city's ordinary routes. Naturally, many of these routes had been Alekseeva's, her husband's, her friends'. I marveled anew, while walking the former Leningrad, the hero city, the survivor city, at how Petersburg itself – its buildings, its landscapes, its inhabitants – has a way of serving as a kind of collective conversational partner, enhancing both interior monologues and dialogues among companions. Alekseeva's poems often hinge on such an interplay of settings and articulated thoughts.

The Institute of the Living Word, where she had studied, had been short-lived, like Alekseeva herself, and like so many of her mentors and associates. Yet the word lived on in the city's world. The lasting influence of the institute and its inimitable instructor Gumilyov is also palpable in the memoirs of Alekseeva's fellow student Irina Odoevtseva, whose *On the Banks of the Neva* our author Tamara Partanenko had made us a timely present of shortly after our arrival.

Alekseeva's own several Gumilyov tributes, all written in the eternal present tense, hauntingly distill living words in action. In the face of bitter loss, the younger poet struggles to reclaim her slain teacher's spirit. As in the case of other students reportedly enthralled with Gumilyov, whether or not a romantic liaison occurred, Alekseeva aims for poetry as a way to make up for interrupted lessons.

In "Ships," the earliest of the three poems translated here, the results of her efforts remain ethereal, inconclusive. The poet seeks less to resurrect Gumilyov than to accept with his terrible end, envisioned as if as one more of his departures to exotic locales, blending the mythology of his bloodlines and sea-tinged youth with archetypes of separation.

In the next two poems, however, written a year later, Gumilyov is vividly present, as larger than life as in life. With an entranced Alekseeva tagging along as an audience of one, in each of these twin variations on a theme, Gumilyov strides through the city declaiming a "poem of poems," end-rhymed in both cases with "Eden," the paradise toward which his incantation forms a vector. A Pied Piper of aesthetics, he seems preemptively beatified by genius, whose luminosity extends beyond his person to his pupil and each landmark of their route. With the master poet "marked by God's hand," the shared inspiration of their impromptu ceremonial processions accrues with no canonical chaperone. The effusive poet's evocation of a world of unshadowed efflorescence stands in bittersweet contrast to his apprentice's registry of personal and observed paucity of spirit, cultivation and good fortune. Seeing the limitations of the poetic art as perhaps merely conditionally proposing pantheistic harmony, Alekseeva remains achingly aware of her teacher's human fallibility, vulnerability, mortality. Each juxtaposed urban yearning mirrors this awareness. At each step of the way, abject and rarefied aspirations alike loom as at once visceral and immaterial. Yet in Alekseeva's compassion, apparent discord finds resolution, with bespattered streets and intuited Eden endowed with an equally real, axial consonance. Amid an agile cosmogony, coaxed toward and craving transcendence, Alekseeva involuntarily, half-ironically identifies with thwarted, compromised specimens of life among her fellow citizens: a fawning mutt, a begging crone, a besotted ragamuffin attaining his own crude lyrical rapture. Acknowledging her "lack of art," recognizing each life's hybrid of sublimity and frailty, Alekseeva, part of the next cultural generation, orphaned by ideological shifts, both mourns the virtuoso and shows her own aptitude for intermingling heaven and earth. Alone, she might be found wanting, but in humbly begging, she might gather enough alms from her forerunners, her environment, the air itself, to survive and to make her own offerings with a dignity reserved for holy fools.

With these translations, groping for equivalents for the originals' eloquent, highly charged simplicity was a slow, sometimes frustrating process. A wish to sob, like Alekseeva and the beggar, was not foreign in this time of uncertainty, not only for artistic reasons and not only due to the bleakness of so much in the poets' odyssey. Our era of Alekseeva was a different time of suffering, of fragility and rawness, but also of an urgency of poetic modes of being, wherever such instincts might lead.

My last completed revision to these translations, yielding the line "And greedy paws at the air,/Seeking ghosts of clinking coins," felt emblematic of our specific journey with Alekseeva, as well as of universal predicaments, of the petty yet precious stakes of destiny. The translated passage had once read "Makes greedy gestures, fumbling in the air/For ghosts of far-off jingling coins." Boris Dralyuk encouraged me to tighten the rhythm throughout the two perambulation poems, with about a metrical foot ultimately shed from each line. "Alekseeva's work is so strong, so striking," he commented, "and I want her to grab anglophone readers by their lapels!" After a flurry of revisions, Dralyuk quipped, "The clinking coins are nearly in hand." The content and act of translation became indistinguishable.

Fittingly, the final touch came in a sudden inspiration to add "Seeking" – as

Dralyuk remarked, "*le mot juste*, which brings with it a hint of tragedy…" Indeed tragedy so abounded in these poems' substance that hints could generally suffic to acknowledge its presence, with touches of levity and exuberance also keepin the tone in proportion. Even if we are perpetually seeking, not necessarily finding and even if we often seek phantoms, poems can "glow in the dark," and not onl because of the poems' own strength, but as evidence of an abiding spirit throug which human impulses can endure and speak beyond the confines of their genesi

Over several seasons, paths of shelter and peregrination with Alekseeva wor many guises: veiled by smoke, or christened by fresh-fallen snow, or succumbin to a slush much as once seeped through Gumilyov's gaping galoshes. Alternatin visages gradually cohered in a picture of engagement. The appeal of the two earlic poets blithely skirting Kazan Cathedral found a counterpoint, on Tatyana's Day i the new year's first month, in entering and lighting candles there. The earthboun volatility of post-revolutionary Petrograd's street life quivered on beneath contem porary veneers – in the rollicking shambles of the Apraksin marketplace acros from our base in Petersburg, in lone buskers of old war ballads and Tsoi on nearb Haymarket Square, in a blue-eyed amputee begging from stumps braced on adja cent pavement, whether powdered, iced or barren.

The pungent, kaleidoscopic witness crystallized in Alekseeva's poems ha found a harbor outside the fray and in broadening circles of sympathy. Peter burg-based OBERIU specialist Yulia Valieva, already familiar with the Alel seev-Askoldov story, has provided a critical link. Valieva had never encountere Alekseeva's poetry, but knew Askoldov had thought highly of his daughter-in-law work. She learned the Pushkin House manuscript department's annual almana had once published an article on Alekseev by the scholar Aleksey Dmitrenko, wl had included a selection of poems and references to the blockade-themed volun of Alekseeva's work. Unexpectedly, nearly two decades later, a follow-up look Alekseev was scheduled for an upcoming issue.

Dmitrenko quotes Askoldov's opinion of Alekseeva, as expressed in a 19: letter: "She has a very, very large poetic gift. I've known for a long time that sl writes perfectly good poetry. But only this autumn she read me two poems th would have been worthy of the pen of one of the great Russian poets, who unfortunately died early, like Lermontov. [...] It grieves me terribly that her and Vova's poetic gifts (almost equal) are disappearing with no chance to be revealed."

Belatedly, more chances for revelation are arriving. Discussions with the head of the manuscript department, T. S. Tsarkova, have led to the Pushkin House's consent to acquire Alekseeva's archive digitally – Piotr feels unready to part with his newfound treasure – and to gradually start publishing Alekseeva's oeuvre as well, perhaps introduced by Valieva. The Alekseevs apparently had a rocky relationship, but their archives and legacies can now reasonably live together. They will be in good company at the Pushkin House, as we saw on an afternoon visit hosted by Tsarkova and highlighted by glimpses of Lermontov's saber, Tolstoy's home-cobbled boots and Dostoevsky's notes for *Brothers Karamazov*.

During our time in St. Petersburg, archivist Sergei Chubraev began organizing the intact materials accumulated from nearly fifty years of cultural activity at our offices there. Branching out from a private collection focused on Sergei Kuryokhin and a panoply of Soviet poets and rock musicians, Chubraev has supported efforts sponsored by the Pushkin House and other organizations seeking to trace Russia's alternative culture in the eras after the Silver Age. With our own once-dusty archives open for shuffling and scrutiny, we returned from work on Alekseeva's behalf with relief and reverence for the meaning of stewardship.

Rather than disappearing, Alekseeva's poetry can enter the canon. At last, experts and readers have a chance to come to terms with her accomplishment. Confronting our own challenges, we need what we can salvage from her example.

Ships
In Memory of N. S. Gumilyov

On the woolen felt, rings of electric sun.
Past the window, mists sow water …
I recall a towheaded Estonian
And the same weather …

     Past the river, city lights are shining,
     Farewell handshakes traded firmly,
     These are ships that won't soon be returning –
     From the Neman, bound for Brooklyn.

On this evening, parting ways feels awful,
Water trickles from a turndown collar …
A bouquet bears a white chamomile
Flower from my sixteenth summer.

     Then a tremor rocks the clumsy steamer,
     In the darkness blows a warning siren.
     My Estonian's an hour from departure
     For his native Neman.

Why, oh why, were they all born to sail,
All your fathers, all your grandfathers,
And why can't the soul be made of stone?
Why are you eternally a drifter?

     If you sail to the Tropic of Capricorn,
     Kiss a chamomile in a bouquet.
     If you fall on the horn of a unicorn,
     Recall a girl who wrote you poetry.

Past the river, city lights are shining,
In the darkness wails a siren,
These are ships that won't soon be returning,
Sailing to the distant Neman …

On the woolen felt, rings of electric sun.
Past the window, mists sow water …
I recall a towheaded Estonian
And the same weather …

August 1922

To a Poet

You stride over Petrograd's puddles
Read aloud the poem of poems,
As if through a garden you ramble
Toward a laughing, gleaming Eden.
And Kazan Cathedral's walls loom
To shade our blooming day,
But that pall won't soon dare touch you,
Won't dim your cloudless gaze.
Eternal joy, lightness, a lifetime
Of simple innocence
Belong to those marked by God's hand,
To those whose lips He has kissed.
That is why, triumphant and modest,
You've journeyed from lands of orange groves,
And think our whole huge city fits
In your pocket like ragged notes.
That is why you gaze with derision
At our sinning's lack of art,
And why, from your first days, you've written
Poems that glow in the dark.

1923

A mangy mutt with tawny-tufted ears
Has looked us in the eye and bolted out
Of alley gates to whine beside our heels
With funny, loping steps, a prancing goat.
And now our walk's a tallying of drunkards,
A smearing of the sidewalk's muck.
A ragamuffin bellows out a shanty,
Grabbing walls to prop himself up.
A poor old crone at each pub door
Again stands watch, purse open,
And greedily paws at the air,
Seeking ghosts of clinking coins.
While you, arms stretching skyward,
Are reading the poem of poems,
Incantations that enchant the heart,
A summons from street mud to Eden.
Beneath your hole-dotted galoshes,
Slush squelches, seeping in,
And I want to join the beggar's sobs,
To seize the air's spare change.

1923

AUTHORS

Anna Akhmatova was born near Odessa in 1889, but lived most of her life in Saint Petersburg. As a consequence of her decision to remain in Russia after the October Revolution she faced much personal hardship and a protracted poetic silence, but was also able to create *Requiem*, her great affirmation of solidarity with the victims of the Stalinist purges. She died in Moscow in 1966.

Anna Alekseeva (1899-1945), a poet on the fringes of post-Revolutionary Russian literature, studied with Nikolai Gumilyov and married poet Vladimir Alekseev, an early friend and collaborator of Alexander Vvedensky. Having lost her husband to the siege of Leningrad and her son to the front, Alekseeva passed away just after the Allied victory. Unpublished in her lifetime, she left behind an extensive body of work, rediscovered in 2020.

Stephen Capus has published poems, translations, and reviews in various magazines, including *Acumen*, *Modern Poetry in Translation*, and *Stand*. His pamphlet *24 Hours* was published by Rack Press in 2020.

Svetlana Evdokimova is a poet and professor of Slavic Studies and Comparative Literature at Brown University. Before coming to Brown in 1991, she held a teaching position at Yale University, where she earned her doctorate in Slavic Languages and Literatures. She has published articles on Pushkin, Gogol, Tolstoy, Dostoevsky, Chekhov and others, is the author of *Alexander Pushkin's Historical Imagination* (Yale University Press, 1999), and is the editor of *Pushkin's Little Tragedies: The Poetics of Brevity* (Wisconsin University Press, 2003) and, with Vladimir Golstein, of *Dostoevsky Beyond Dostoevsky: Science, Aesthetics, Religion* (Academic Studies Press, 2016). Her book *Staging Existence: Chekhov's Tetralogy* will appear from Wisconsin University Press. Her poems have appeared in the journals *Zvezda*, *Neva*, and *Severnaya Avrora*, and have been translated into Bulgarian. A collection of her verse, *Amplitudo Cordis*, was published by Vremia in Moscow in 2020.

Homero Freitas de Andrade (1952-2020) was a writer, translator, and professor of literature at the University of São Paulo, Brazil. He was awarded prizes for his Portuguese translations of Chekhov and Pirandello.

Veniamin Gushchin is a PhD candidate at Columbia University. His translations of Vladimir Mayakovsky have won the Columbia University Slavic Department Pushkin Prize. *Blockade Swallow*, his translations of selected poems by Olga Bergolts, is forthcoming from Smokestack Books in spring 2022.

Zsuzsa Hetényi is a Professor of Russian Literature at ELTE, Budapest, who has been awarded Belletrist Prize (2020) and, for literary translation, the Füst Milán Prize (2002). Hetenyi's main fields of research are Russian prose of the twentieth century, questions of identity, emigration and bilingualism in literature, and the practical theory of translation.

Anna J. Jasinska is a molecular geneticist (MSc in Molecular Biology, PhD in Biochemistry). Born in Szczecin, Poland, she studied and worked in Poznań, and since 2005 has been living and working in Los Angeles. Her poems have appeared in *California Quarterly* and *Oddball*, and have received honorable mentions (New Poet and Spanish Language) in the Oregon Poetry Association's contest.

Sara Jolly is a literary translator based in London. Her translations include Igor Golomstock's memoirs, *A Ransomed Dissident, A Life in Art under the Soviets* (I. B. Tauris/Bloomsbury, 2018), Alexander Etkind's *Nature's Evil: A Cultural History of Natural Resources* (Polity, 2021), and short stories in Teffi's *Other Worlds, Pilgrims, Peasants, Spirits, Saints* (Pushkin Press and NYRB Classics, 2021), edited by Robert Chandler.

Kevin Kearney, a writer of fiction, poetry and literary translations, was born on May 27, 1957 in Sunnyside, WA, and studied English and German literature at Stanford University (1975-1979), followed by French language and literature studies in Aix-en-Provence, France (1981-1982), and an MBA at Insead (1984) in Fontainebleau, France. His fiction and poetry have appeared in literary magazines including *Orbis International Literary Journal* and *The New Renaissance*. He spent nearly three decades as an IT executive in Europe for Hewlett-Packard, with major emphasis on building up the company's presence in the new democracies of Central and Eastern Europe (after 1989), including Russia, Poland, the Czech Republic, Hungary, and Slovakia. He is most recently active as a graduate student in Earth Sciences at the University of Vienna in Austria, where he currently resides with his wife of thirty-six years.

James Manteith is a translator, writer, and musician. He serves as contributing translation editor for *Apraksin Blues* and as editorial advisor for Mundus Artium Press. His mentorship with Tatyana Apraksina has informed his translation of her *California Psalms* (Radiolarian), as well as his other interdisciplinary explorations.

Adam Mickiewicz, Poland's national poet, was born on December 24, 1798, in Zaosye, near Nowogródek (now Navahrudak, Belarus), in the Russian Empire, and died on November 26, 1855, in Istanbul (formerly Constantinople), Turkey. Mickiewicz belonged to an impoverished noble family and studied at the University of Wilno (now Vilnius University) between 1815 and 1819. A lifelong crusader for Polish independence, he joined various covert political organizations as a student. He was arrested in 1823 for illegal patriotic activities and deported to Russia, which was the start of a life of permanent exile from his home country. In Moscow, he made the acquaintance of Aleksandr Pushkin and other Russian intellectuals. His trip to Crimea in 1825 became the catalyst for a cycle of sonnets which were published in 1826.

Alexei Nikitin was born in Kyiv in 1967. After completing his course of physics at the University of Kyiv and his period of conscription he established his own company in 1992 and worked on different projects for the Ukrainian oil, chemical and atomic industries. In 2002 Niktin closed his business operations and worked for several years as an IT journalist. Afterwards he dedicated himself completely to his literary activities and has since published several novels: *Istemi* (2011), *Madzhong* (2012), *Victory Park* (2013) *Sanitar s Institutskoi* (2016), and, most recently, *Ot litsa ognia* (2021). He has received several literary awards and is one of the most prominent Russian-language writers in Ukraine today. Alexei Nikitin lives in Kyiv.

Catherine O'Neil is a literary scholar and professor of Russian language and culture at the United States Naval Academy. She has written on Alexander Pushkin and Russian and European romanticism. She has translated Polish poet Juliusz Słowacki in a bilingual edition of *Agamemnon's Tomb*. *Victory Park* is her first attempt at a literary translation of an entire novel. She spent several happy months in Kyiv this past year – accidentally renting an apartment, in fact, in the very building that is featured in this chapter: a twelve-story high-rise, assembled in a semi-circle. She believes in Total Immersion Translation.

Avril Pyman is Reader Emerita in Russian Literature at the University of Durham, UK, and a Fellow of the British Academy. She is an expert in Russian literature of the Silver Age and has published a major biography of Aleksandr Blok (Oxford University Press, 2 volumes, 1979-80) and *A History of Russian Symbolism* (Cambridge University Press, 1994), as well as many translations from Russian. She met the artist Kirill Konstantinovich Sokolov (1930-2004), whose grandmother remembered Blok, in Russia and married him in the autumn of 1963. Their daughter Irina was born in 1965, and the family came to England in 1974.

Ivan Sokolov-Mikitov (1882-1975) was a memoirist, traveler, novelist, and naturalist in the tradition of Sergey Aksakov and Mikhail Prishvin. Before becoming a writer he served in the Imperial Army during the First World War and flew early Russian bomber aircraft.

Irina Steinberg was born in Moscow in 1983. She emigrated to England with her family at the age of eight and now lives primarily in London. She was a co-translator of Teffi's *Subtly Worded and Other Stories* (Pushkin Press, 2014) and *Memories: From Moscow to the Black Sea* (Pushkin Press and NYRB Classics, 2016), which received the Read Russia Prize in 2018, and of Irina Odoevsteva's *Isolde* (Pushkin Press, 2019). Her translations have also appeared in *Russian Émigré Short Stories from Bunin to Yanovsky* (Penguin Classics, 2017), edited by Bryan Karetnyk, and in *Asymptote*. She and Sara Jolly have collaborated on an as yet unpublished translation of Polina Zherebtsova's collection of short stories, *A Fine Silver Thread*.

Gaither Stewart is a journalist and writer. His articles have appeared in the European press, his short stories in various literary magazines, and his short story collections and novels in books published in the United States and Europe. He has lived his adult life in Europe and lives today in Rome, Italy, with his wife Milena.

Evsey Tseytlin is a prominent Russian-born culturologist, writer, literary critic, and scholar. Prior to the collapse of the USSR, he was a member of the Soviet

Writers' Union and taught college courses on literature and cultural history. For the past fifteen years he has been editor of a Chicago-based newspaper. His books have been published in Russia, the United States, Lithuania, and Germany.

Kevin Windle is an Emeritus Professor at the Australian National University. His major publications include *The Oxford Handbook of Translation Studies* (co-edited with Kirsten Malmkjær) and a biography of Alexander Zuzenko. For his translations from various languages he has received international awards.

Lena Wolf was born in Latvia but grew up in Soviet Kazakhstan as a German child of a deported family. Currently based in London, she has lived and worked in New Zealand and Germany, where her family immigrated in 1990. Wolf's ancestors moved to the Russian Empire from Germany 250 years ago. They lived in German villages in Southern Russia and Ukraine, where they owned and farmed land. In 1941 Wolf's whole family was deported to Kazakhstan, where they lived in special settlements as people with no rights until 1956. Her grandmother was sent to the Gulag in Vorkuta for twenty years when she tried to escape the special settlement. Her son, Wolf's father, was sent to an orphanage for children of the enemies of the state. It took Wolf's grandmother almost a decade to find her son. All of Wolf's stories are about what it means to be a German child of a deported family and to live in a country that is hostile to you – a country that is traumatized by the effect of the Second World War, where people use the words "German" and "fascist" interchangeably. And yet, this country is her only home.

Antony Wood is a publisher and a translator from Russian and German. His independent imprint Angel Classics is devoted to translations from European languages. His own translation of Pushkin's *Mozart and Salieri* was read on Radio by Paul Scofield and Simon Callow on publication in 1982; his translation of the uncensored 1825 version of *Boris Godunov* was staged in Princeton in 2007. His wide-ranging *Selected Poetry* of Pushkin, published by Penguin Classics in 2020 won both Read Russia translation prizes awarded by the Institute of Translation Moscow, for that year.

Polina Zherebtsova was born in Grozny in 1985 and grew up in a family of mixed ethnic, linguistic, and cultural heritage. She was nine when the first of the Chechen wars began, prompting her to start keeping a diary. She wrote many volumes of diaries over the next ten years, spanning several more armed conflicts in Chechnya. At the age of fourteen she was wounded by shrapnel during a missile attack by Russian forces on the Central Market. In 2005 Zherebtsova and her mother were finally able to leave Chechnya as refugees. Zherebtsova moved to Moscow with assistance from the Solzhenitsyn Foundation and began working as a journalist. Zherebtsova's childhood diaries, *Ant in a Jar, Chechen Diaries 1994-2004*, were published in Russian in 2011 and attracted great acclaim, but also much hostile attention, including persistent claims that they were fakes. She and her husband claimed political asylum in Finland, where they have been living since 2012. Her collection of stories, *A Fine Silver Thread*, which includes the story "We're Terror-ists," reworks her childhood experiences in fictional form.

PRE-SUBMISSION GUIDELINES
FOR TRANSLATED POETRY
Boris Dralyuk

Before sending poetic translations to Cardinal Points, think about your audience. Our intended reader is a person sensitive to English as it is spoken, susceptible to the effects of verse, and at least somewhat familiar with the Anglophone poetic tradition. These are the people who browse through the poetry shelves at the local bookstore, who open literary journals and flip to the poetry section, who see a box of text with an unjustified right margin in their newspaper and consider giving it a read. In other words, any poetic translation you choose to send out into the world must be good English – and good English verse, at that.

Things to avoid:

1. Unnatural phrasing. If one can't imagine a native English-speaker saying a certain phrase to another native English-speaker, then the phrase must go.
2. Poetic inversions (at least when translating most post-eighteenth-century poetry).
3. Padding to fill out metrical lines.
4. Forced rhymes.

Many translators of Russian poetry believe it their duty to hew closely to a poem's original form. It serves to remember that, to today's Anglophone reader (and not just today's, really), the persistent use of exact rhyme produces a comic effect, especially when coupled with a clangorous short-lined meter like the trochaic tetrameter. If you want your translations to appeal to Anglophone readers, consider loosening the metrical grip – which doesn't necessarily mean abandoning meter, just playing closer attention to rhythm, diversifying the lines, leaving some ictuses unfilled. The original meters are often a trap: they don't mean the same thing for an Anglophone reader as they do for a Russian, with the trochaic tetrameter being a case in point. If you find that you need to add words in order "to fill out" a line, then your line is too long. And don't contort natural syntax in order to fit a rhyme scheme.

The *StoSvet Press* publishing house is a part of the US-based
StoSvet literary project,
which also includes the Стороны *Света / Storony Sveta*
and *Cardinal Points* literary journals, the «Union "I"» web portal,
the annual Oleg Woolf Memorial Reading Series,
and annual Compass Translation Award.

Founding Director: Oleg Woolf (1954-2011)
Editor-in-Chief: Irina Mashinski
www.StoSvet.net

One can order this or other books published by StoSvet Press directly from
its web-site www.stosvet.net/lib/ or by sending an e-mail to info@StoSvet.net

Printed in Great Britain
by Amazon